# When Your Heart Seeks the Sky

## by

## Wang Jian

authorHOUSE

*1663 Liberty Drive, Suite 200*
*Bloomington, Indiana 47403*
*(800) 839-8640*
*www.authorhouse.com*

*First published by AuthorHouse 10/09/04*

*ISBN: 1-4184-8598-5 (sc)*

*Printed in the United States of America*
*Bloomington, Indiana*

*This book is printed on acid-free paper.*

# Acknowledgments

On a spring afternoon shortly after Easter, still feeling the wonderful power of God in my heart from the Easter service I had attended, I decided to sit down and express my thanks to all of you who supported me through the wondrous journey of writing this book. To all of you, I bestow my sincere thanks and blessings.

First, I wish to thank my long time mentor, Mary Anne Thomas. When I became discouraged midway through writing my book, and almost lost hope after experiencing some sharp criticism, Mary Anne sent me a simple note expressing her firm belief in my work. That note inspired me to continue my writing, and is the reason you hold this book in your hands today.

I am also grateful to two special people who supported me and gave me valuable advice during the writing of my book. Thanks to M. Rachel Plummer for editing my work and making the writing sparkle, and to Colleen Szot for compiling my marketing message and making it easy to share this story with others.

I love books, and am very grateful to Joel Christopher, Joe Vitale, Cody Horton, Thomas L. Pauley, Penelope J. Pauley, Cindy Cashman, Lynn Grabhorn, Alan Cohen, Mary Anne Thomas, and Richard Shiningthunder Francis for presenting me with autographed copies of theirs. Thank you for all the blessings that inspired me to follow my dream. Alan, what you wrote on the title page brought tears to my eyes.

Thanks to Robert G. Allen and Mark Victor Hansen for enrolling me in the One Minute Millionaire program. I will never forget the moment I received the huge package of learning materials and became one of their protégés.

I am also grateful to Jack Canfield and Mark Victor Hansen for their fabulous *Chicken Soup for the Soul* series, which taught me to live my dream no matter what happens or how often I might fail.

Special thanks to Og Mandino, Cynthia Kersey, Robert H. Schuller, Jerrold R. Jenkins and Mardi Link. Their masterpieces painted the road to a wonderland of writing before my eyes.

I was thrilled to see Lance Armstrong on television winning the France Tour five times on behalf of the USPS team. You deserve the yellow jersey, Lance, and you are my hero!

Christopher Reeve taught me how to become a superman in real life. You are my star!

Donghua Li gave up so much to make one dream come true. At last he received the Olympic gold medal for the Swiss. Donghua, you are a true man.

I also wish to honor several friends who read my work when it was newly completed, and gave me warm comments, enlightening feedback, and great testimonials: Cody Horton, Mike Dooley, Michael Levy, Josh Hinds, Lee Silber, Toni Graeme, Dr. Joe Rubino, Debbie Call, Michele Blood, Carol Tuttle, Swamy Swarna, John Harricharan, Bonnie Ross-Parker, Naseem Mariam, Richard S. Francis, Stacey Hall, Jan Brogniez, Wayne F. Perkins, Cheryl Wright, Lynn Pierce, Dr. Al Lippart, Colleen Szot, Shirley Cheng, George W. Ludwig, Eric J. Aronson, Rie Sheridan, Dan Poynter, Thomas L Pauley and William Homeier.

A special note of gratitude to Linda Stafford, who reminded me in her speech—I never Write Right—that anybody could become a writer if he wanted it badly enough.

I would like to express my sincere thanks to Susan Miller of Astrology Zone, who encouraged me to turn my thoughts into words and, finally, a published book.

A special thanks to my longtime friends, Les Ely and Karla Ely, for their support in my growing faith, and for all their prayers that I gain unwavering belief in God's love.

I further wish to thank Ingrid Smith. The letter she wrote me is on my desk to remind me of the warm blessing she sent from across the country.

To readers all over the world, I send my deepest love and best wishes. Without your support and warm feedback, I couldn't have achieved my writing success. I wanted to write a story to inspire you to reach for your dreams and live the life you love. Thank you for reading this book and sharing it with your family and friends. Love can move world!

To my mother and father, who offered me their invaluable power and wisdom throughout my life. Thank you, Mom, for teaching me many lessons about living a happy and wonderful life that I could never learn in school. Thank you, Dad, for giving me *The Wonderful Adventures of Nils* when I was pupil and opening the secret gate of great literature for me. I thank you both for your continuous encouragement and unfailing belief that someday this book would be published. My prayers and thanks are with you.

At last, thank you, God, for leading me every step of the way and showing me the light inside the darkness. "Oh, that You would bless me indeed, and enlarge my territory, that Your hand would be with me, and You would keep me from evil, that I may not cause pain!" Please help to spread the word of this sweet story with your hand and touch millions of people all over the world.

God bless us all!

# Advance Praise for *When Your Heart Seeks the Sky*

"*When Your Heart Seeks the Sky* is a very spiritual and awe-inspiring story. Wang Jian has put his thoughts to pen in a way that no one else can. The book is timeless and is written so poetically that people of all ages will enjoy it! On a scale from one to ten this book is definitely a ten! Thank you Wang Jian."
—Cody Horton, Author of Consciously Creating Wealth

"A touching story that reminds its readers of what's really important in life: family, friends, and following your heart!"
—Mike Dooley, Author of Totally Unique Thoughts

"*When Your Heart Seeks the Sky* is an inspirational story written in a simple manner and that is the art and hallmark of a good writer. Wang Jian has captured the spirit of his story and allows the reader to fly away into the realms of authentic living. I recommend *When Your Heart Seeks the Sky* to all folks who wish to fly with their soul."
—Michael Levy, Author of Invest With a Genius

"This is a wonderful tale of reaching for, and achieving ones dreams. Experience the trials, and successes of Dodo as he sets out to live the life he was meant to live. This book should be part of the success library of anyone that wishes to set out on the journey of living a life filled with much success and happiness."
—Josh Hinds, Author of A Journey of Inspiration

"Who would have thought we could learn life lessons from a chicken? However, Wang Jian found a way to weave timeless tips throughout *When Your Heart Seeks the Sky*."
—Lee Silber, Award-Winning Author of Self-Promotion For The Creative Person

"A charming and entertaining story for children, easy to read to them or, for them to read themselves. Featuring animals for people, this philosophical tale tells of lessons we can learn about accepting ourselves and rising to challenges as we come to know ourselves and believe in our own self and what we want to be. Wang Jian also tells of the importance to realize we

are not alone and can ask for and accept offered help from others around us who are ready to give. Wang Jian gives us a colourful setting with visual descriptive passages. Children will love the animals, understand their difficulties and be delighted with the exciting ending. The main character shows encouragement and support for young readers who may need it"
>   ——Toni Graeme, Publisher of Women Who Lived and
>   Loved North of 60

"*When Your Heart Seeks the Sky* by Wang Jian is an uplifting and moving fable that speaks to overcoming life's challenges. It is a heart-warming story about the power of love, appropriate for young and older readers alike."
>   ——Dr. Joe Rubino, Best-selling Author of *The
>   Magic Lantern: A Fable About Leadership,Personal
>   Excellence and Empowerment*

"Wang Jian's fable, *When Your Heart Seeks the Sky,* resonates with the power of truth. It reminds us that the heart knows the way. By following its wisdom, the heart also guides us in finding the courage to stay the course. Delightful and inspiring! "
>   ——Debbie Call, Author of *Tug of Heart - How to Trust
>   What You Know*

"*When Your Heart Seeks the Sky* by Wang Jian is a beautiful book that metaphors the truth of who we really are inside. You will learn in such a beautiful story how when we are persistent we will see the beauty that is inside of us all. You will learn that to become the leader who makes his own fortune is far better than a follower who does nothing. You will see that inside of us all is a beautiful eagle no matter what we think we are. You will learn that even when we begin to see the eagle within we still must learn to fly. And fly you will to places that you could only dream of. If you loved "*Jonathan Livingston Seagull*" you will adore this book."
>   ——Michele Blood, Producer and TV show host of
>   MPowerTV.com and Author of the MusiVation
>   metaphysical product line.

"*When Your Heart Seeks the Sky* is a wonderful story that will touch you deeply. Wang Jian has written it purely and thoughtfully. Well done!"
>   ——Carol Tuttle, Author of *Remembering Wholeness*

"Very heart-warming. Highly symbolic and spiritual.

*When Your Heart Seeks the Sky* by Wang Jian is a fabulous book, the story of how a spirit finds its true nature. Written as a fable, it is the moving and heartwarming story of a bald eagle, who was raised as a chicken, but who finds his true nature and regains his rightful place in Gods creation. A very heart warming story, it has all the elements that touch you, all the values that help you find your true self.

This book is a good read for children of all ages, since there is always a child in each of us, a child, who had dreams, whose dreams have not yet become a reality. It is the birth right of every soul to dream, but to make the dream a reality, one has to take the trouble of going through a spiritual renewal, a painful but necessary process. Wang Jian holds your attention at every page, nay, every line.

Read it for simple entertainment, if you prefer. But read it, with sincerity, read it between the lines, for the real message of spiritual renewal, that the book is really about. And then, go for it. Go for fulfilling your own dream! Learn to soar!"

> ——Swamy Swarna, Writer, Editor, Proof Reader and
> Independent Book Reviewer

"Wang Jian's book, '*When the Heart Seeks the Sky*' is a masterful blend of fable and eternal truths. I started reading it one evening and could not put it down until the last word. This book is a brilliant testimony to the true power that resides in the soul of each and every one of us. Read it and let the characters speak to your heart. You'll be all the better for it.

> —John Harricharan, award-winning author of the
> bestseller, "*When You Can Walk on Water, Take the Boat*"

"Author Wang Jian has created a masterpiece in "*When Your Heart Seeks The Sky*". He weaves powerful lessons into a memorable fable causing the reader to search within to determine whether or not he or she is fulfilling his or her own destiny. His core message 'Always live the life you want to live' is felt throughout."

> ——Bonnie Ross-Parker, Author, "*Walk In My Boots - The
> Joy of Connecting*"

"Wang Jian's book "*When Your Heart Seeks the Sky*" describes a chick becoming an eagle. The process of change brings with it pain, anxiety and finally triumph. Wang Jian does a very good job in describing in detail the feelings, thoughts and actions that the protagonist goes through. This is especially relevant in today's context where many people find a need to re-engineer themselves to be more employable: adjusting to a new workplace, starting a new venture. The lines I liked the most in the book: "The ability you must master is not only how to flap your wings to rise in the air, but also how to glide on the wind, becoming part of it." And "always go against the wind". This is so true of life: a combination of confrontation and acquiescence is required to achieve success. This advice is similar to applying the Serenity Prayer: "God, Grant me the serenity to accept the things I cannot change, the courage to change the things I can, and the wisdom to know the difference." Wang Jian's book is a must read for those who wish to better develop their personalities. It is written in a simple, clear language and is a suitable read for both children and adults."

——Naseem Mariam, Project Management Coach

"This is a delightful story of charming characters who show the great power of love and courage. It is at once cute, whimsical, and most entertaining."

——Richard S Francis, Author of *Falling in Love with Yourself*

"A delightfully attractive story."

——Stacey Hall and Jan Brogniez, co-authors
"*Attracting Perfect Customers…The Power of Strategic Synchronicity*"

"Brilliant work Wang Jian, on "*When Your Heart Seeks The Sky*." Be prepared for a sensitive story, enabling you to find your motivation to overcome your present condition in life. Wang Jian weaves valuable metaphors, in a wonderful story, with lessons, you and your entire family will enjoy. If you want to find your mission in life, and when you want to find your passion, "*When Your Heart Seeks The Sky*," will take your spirits to the heavens."

——Wayne F. Perkins, Hypnotist and Sales Trainer

"Wang Jian's *When Your Heart Seeks The Sky* is replete with crisp characterizations. It makes for pleasant bedtime reading for young children. Yet it is stimulating enough to be used as a literature text for junior and senior high school. It has great potential to be a Disney movie for the whole family."

——Cheryl Wright, interior design consultant and freelance writer

"This is an amazing story that pulls you in so quickly you don't want to miss one word. What a beautiful picture Wang Jian paints of Dodo's triumphant rise from chicken to eagle. Filled with so many lessons for adults and children alike, you'll get goose bumps and tears in your eyes as Dodo realizes his destiny. This is a must read for anyone who needs a reminder of why you must continue to go for your dream."

—Lynn Pierce, #1 Best Selling Co-Author of "*Wake-up...Live the Life You Love*"

"*When Your Heart Seeks the Sky*" is an engaging "Ugly Duckling" story with a powerful intellectual twist. Through animal analogies, the author, teaches that it is never too late to be what you were meant to be. You are never too old to pursue your dreams, if you are willing to pay the price. And if you love and know animals as I do, you realize that animals and animal stories can not only teach and entertain us, but they can also inspire us to live happier and more fulfilling lives.

—Dr. Al Lippart, Veterinarian, Author of *SMARTER Success*

"I love *When Your Heart Seeks the Sky* - it's a story of giving and love and family, one that every person can learn from."

—Colleen Szot, Writer

"A truly heartwarming tale of courage and determination, *When Your Heart Seeks the Sky* by Wang Jian, provokes the readers to reach for the stars to achieve their dreams—no matter what obstacle and hardship may block the way. With lovable animal characters, this tale tells the story of a young eagle, Dodo, going for his dream of being a true eagle. Raised as a chicken, Dodo must master the true way of living life as his own kind. And learning how to fly is not the only lesson that he needs to learn—there are the deeper meanings of being a true eagle. Wang Jian, a talented author, gives a strong message through his fable. This easy-to-read book is a wonderful read full of encouragement and inspiration, and is suited for all ages and cultures. It states a universal message: to never give up on your dreams and hopes. Although the road may be thorny and rough, there is always light at the end of the dark tunnel. I highly recommend it and give it five stars."

—Shirley Cheng, author of *Daring Quests of Mystics*

"*When Your Heart Seeks the Sky* is a moving story that touches the heart and sparks a passion to pursue your dreams."

    —George W. Ludwig, Bestselling Author, *Wise Moves and Power Selling*

"You will be delighted and surprised as you read this incredibly unique, creative and wise masterpiece. This phenomenal book will inspire and encourage you to live your life at your highest potential. You'll want to share this with everyone you love and care about."

    —Peggy McColl, Author of "*On Being a Dog with a Bone*"

"The Book has many messages, some clearly apparent and some slightly surreptitious. I found the book to be inspirational and a quick read. With so many messages that are subliminally implemented into you subconscious, you can relate to the many struggles that one must go through in order to survive what life gives you. The reader can never grow tired of the core message, "follow your dreams". Dodo has taught me a lesson or two that I will never forget."

    —Eric J. Aronson, Author of *Dash*

"*When Your Heart Seeks the Sky* is a charming fable celebrating the strength to dream. Dodo has been raised as a chicken, but when he finds his true destiny is to soar with the eagles, he must find the courage to take to the sky. The lesson is a simple one, but one that never gets old — dare to follow your heart, even when it seeks the sky."

    —Rie Sheridan, Author of RieVisions and The Right Hand of Velachaz

"People love stories and they are a great way to convey an inspirational message. You will find both this story and the message irresistible."

    —Dan Poynter, *The Self-Publishing Manual*

"Your book is the picture of perseverance."

    —Thomas L Pauley, Author of *I'm Rich Beyond My Wildest Dreams*

"Whether young or young at heart, or even one who may have but a shadow of your life's dreams still within, "When Your Heart Seek the Sky" will awaken from even the deepest slumber, and encourage you to life from your heart with enthusiasm. This wonderful story calls to the best in each of us. Live life fully, live well, and soar like an eagle."

——William Homeier，Song Writer/ Singer/Speaker

If you bought this for a friend, please send a blessing to them here.

To contact the author of this book,
please email author@heartseeks.com
or visit his website at www.heartseeks.com
To order more copies of this book
for your friends and family,
please visit www.amazon.com
or www.bn.com
search book title
When Your Heart Seeks the Sky

To My Mother and Father,
who show me love

with all their hearts

## Effective Prayer

7"Keep on asking, and you will be given what you ask for. Keep on looking, and you will find. Keep on knocking, and the door will be opened. 8For everyone who asks, receives. Everyone who seeks, finds. And the door is opened to everyone who knocks. 9You parents—if your children ask for a loaf of bread, do you give them a stone instead? 10Or if they ask for a fish, do you give them a snake? Of course not! 11If you sinful people know how to give good gifts to your children, how much more will your heavenly Father give good gifts to those who ask him.

## The Golden Rule

12"Do for others what you would like them to do for you. This is a summary of all that is taught in the law and the prophets.

Matthew 7:7-12

# Chapter 1

It was a rainy summer afternoon. Seven-year-old Dodo left school with his chicken classmates after the rain stopped. The great land in the Western Forest was brighter and clearer after the shower. Uncle Sun smiled happily in the sky. Water droplets glistened like diamonds on the green grass and the body of locusts. The air was full of the sweet scent of flowers and grass, and all the chickens ran and laughed, happy to breathe the fresh air after a boring day in school.

"Hey, buddy! Let's play the locust-catching game, OK?" Bipa suggested to his friends. All the chickens stopped singing and turned to look at Bipa.

"Yay!" The chickens jumped for joy because they were about to take their afternoon tea, and locusts would be a delicious treat. It would also be fun just to play the game.

"But we have to follow the rules this time," Bipa added.

The last time they played, many of their classmates broke the rules and nobody was crowned the winner.

"Okay. What are the rules? Hurry, hurry, hurry!" The chickens couldn't wait another minute, they were so excited. Their mouths watered at the idea of having tasty locusts with their tea.

"Let me think a minute." Bipa blinked, mulling it over. "The chicken who gets the first locust will win the game. How does that sound?"

"No, no, no," cried the other chickens. "That won't work."

"But why?" Bipa didn't understand why his wonderful suggestion was being rejected.

"Because, Bipa," said Dodo, "who will know if someone catches the first locust if the locust is already eaten?"

"Ah yes, you're right." Bipa looked thoughtful. "Do you have a better idea?"

All the chickens lowered their heads in thought. But they couldn't think of anything better than Bipa's suggestion.

Then Dodo raised his head. "I have an idea," he said, rubbing his sharp beak against his long feathers. Feathers that were so much longer than the other chickens'.

"Quick, tell us," said Bipa, his own short wings beating anxiously. "I'm hungry."

"OK," replied Dodo. "We could eat a few of the locusts we catch, but wait and save the rest of them to count. Who ever catches ten locusts first wins the game."

"Wow! That's a great idea," Bipa said.

"Yeah. Not only will we have tasty locusts with our afternoon tea, but also someone gets to win the game because we have some rules to follow this time."

"OK. Are you ready? Wait for the count…" Bipa warned.

The chickens stood in line and waited for Bipa to count to three. Their hearts pounded as they got ready to hunt in the deep grass.

"One…" Bipa began. "Two… three. Let's go." Then Bipa, Dodo and the other chickens rushed into the thick wet grass to find their food.

It is hard to find locusts after a rain shower. They are the same color as the grass, and the drops of water hide them even more. But all the chickens were trained in school to keep a sharp eye out for their food, so Bipa and the other chickens hurried along the same route, searching out locusts.

Only Dodo hung behind. *Why not find somewhere the others aren't looking?* he thought. *The locusts will hide in their holes after seeing so many chickens. Only the small and sickly locusts will be left to eat. But if I stay here, I can capture the escaping locusts before they can hide.*

Dodo waited patiently until the escaping locusts flew his way. "One, two, three," he counted, grabbing the locusts with his sharp beak and gobbling them down. "Wow! These are so delicious!"

He was about to eat the third locust, when he realized that he would lose the game if he ate all his locusts before they were counted. "OK, I'll eat you later," he told the struggling insect. Then he scratched a mark in the locust's back so he could distinguish it from the others.

"Six, seven, eight," he continued, capturing more locusts.

Meanwhile, Bipa had seen what Dodo was doing and hurried to capture some of the fleeing locusts. He had nine when he and Dodo dove for the same locust, banging their heads together. "Ow!" Bipa cried, and Dodo managed to grab the locust first.

"I win, I win, I win." he shouted to the sky, ignoring the pain in his head.

The other chickens stopped their search.

"Unbelievable," said one.

"Wow," said another.

Soon, every chicken had congratulated the new winner.

Dodo shook his wings and head happily, and forgot about his headache. He was so happy, he even neglected to eat the rest of his delicious locusts!

But his happiness didn't last long. "Dodo isn't the winner." Bipa declared, surprising the other chickens into a stunned silence. "Dodo cheated!"

"What?" said Dodo, shocked by Bipa's accusation.

All the chickens stopped, anxious to hear what Bipa had to say.

"You lied," Bipa said. "The tenth locust is mine. I caught it first." Then Bipa showed the crowd his entire nine locusts. "Now," he said to Dodo. "Show me *your* locusts."

Dodo handed the ten locusts to Bipa. Bipa checked everyone carefully and cried, "Hey, this one is a dead locust. Ha-ha." He pointed to the third locust out to the crowd, turning slowly so all the chickens could examine it. It was the locust Dodo had marked. The scratch had gone deep, and the locust had died of the wound.

"No. It was alive when I caught it," Dodo said. "I just scratched a line in its back so I could distinguish it from others."

"Yet there's no blood on your claw," Bipa said with an evil smile. "If you scratched the locust when it was alive, there should be blood on your claw. Therefore, I say that Dodo is a big liar."

All the chickens looked down at Dodo's claws. Both were clean and clear, without a drop of blood. They began to whisper amongst themselves.

Suddenly, Bipa began to sing a song they had all learned in school, except he changed the words. "Big wing Dodo, ugly face Dodo," he sang. "Big liar Dodo, ugly face Dodo."

"No, no. Bipa isn't telling the truth." Dodo protested to the crowd. But his words were lost as the rest of the chickens took up Bipa's song. "Big wing Dodo, ugly face Dodo. Big liar Dodo, ugly face Dodo." The crowd of chickens began to throw mud at Dodo. They bit the long feathers on his wings, singing louder and louder.

Dodo huddled low to avoid the other chickens' attack. At the same time, he begged, "Please trust me. I'm not a liar." But it was useless. Nobody would listen. They just kept singing the "Big liar" song with Bipa.

At last, Dodo shook the mud from his feathers and ran as fast as an arrow back to his home, crying all the way.

"Mom, mom. Where are you?" he cried when he reached his house.

Dodo's mother was cooking dinner in the kitchen. She rushed into living room to see what happened when she heard the desperation in Dodo's voice.

"Hey, my baby. What's the matter?" She was very surprised when she saw the mud on his long wings and the tears running down his cheeks. Some of his feathers were even broken.

"Mom," Dodo cried. "My classmates called me a big liar. They said I cheated at the locust game. They threw mud at me and made up a song about 'big liar and ugly face.'" Dodo rushed into his mother's arms and sobbed.

Tada put her feathers on Dodo's wing, brushed off the rest of the mud, and hugged Dodo tightly until he calmed down.

After a while, held next to Tada's warm bosom, listening to her heart, Dodo said, "Why do I have long wings and a sharp beak while the others have short wings and a straight beak?"

"Oh, my baby," Tada replied. "Every chicken looks different from every other chicken. No one has the same face as the other. Please remember that we all are unique, and never judge a chicken by his looks. It is God who gives us our features, and He has His reasons, which we may not know. But there is a meaning to everything. You are not ugly, but you are different. Everybody is beautiful in God's eyes. Ugliness comes from the chickens themselves. When someone thinks ugly thoughts, they see ugly things. Always remember that you are unique in the world.

"And remember this, little one, your appearance will help you later on." Tada smiled at her son. "Remember, too, that you are stronger and braver because you have two long wings and a sharp beak. So you can catch locusts faster than your classmates and win the game."

Dodo felt better. He even forgot the painful bites on his wings. He began to like his long wings and sharp beak a bit. He used to wish that he looked like the rest of his classmates, but he didn't mind looking different so much now.

"Go take a bath, now," Tada said. "Then we'll eat supper."

Tada released Dodo from her grasp and began to prepare the dinner table, while Dodo soaked in a tub of hot water and let the past fly far from his mind.

After a good dinner, where Dodo talked about his school day, it was time for bed and a bedtime story. Dodo recalled the afternoon game and asked Tada one question before she picked up the picture book. "Why do the other chickens always make fun of the way I look?"

"Because…" Tada thought for a second, then began again. "There are two kinds of people in the chicken family," she declared. "Only two."

"What do you mean?" Dodo asked, puzzled, wondering what this had to do with the other chickens making fun of him.

"There are the leaders and followers," Tada replied. "The leader is the director for the whole chicken family. He is the master of the group. He leads us wherever we go. He is the master of his own fortune and the only person to decide his own destiny."

"The rest are followers. Everybody follows the leader. They don't know what to do or where to go unless the leader tells them. Which means they don't make their own future. They let others decide their future for them. Followers are nobody.

"Do you think that leaders are born leaders?" Tada continued. "Absolutely not. The person who overcomes the most difficulties and still stands tall in the crowd will become the head of all the chickens. He must be able to protect the whole group and provide us safety and abundant food. He will have to withstand everybody's criticism, and humbly accept their praises now and then. Because he is somebody, the others will talk about him. They will love him or hate him, but always, always they will talk about him. Just like they talk about our leader, Hera.

"The chickens will never talk about a follower chicken because he is nobody. They don't bother to criticize him or praise him. Ever. It doesn't matter what people say about you—the fact that they are talking means you are better than the others. By standing out enough so others talk about you, you will become the leader.

"So, do you want to become the leader who makes your own fortune or a follower who does nothing?"

"I want to become like Hera," Dodo said. Dodo very much admired Hera, who was the strongest and bravest chicken in the whole family.

"Then your fortune begins," Tada said. And she put down the picture book and turned off the lights in Dodo's room. And Dodo, drifting off to sleep, had no idea that this was the first of many such talks that would change his life forever.

# **Chapter 2**

Two years later, Dodo had grown into a strong, young chicken. He had also become very thoughtful, thinking about many things in his spare time. He was very surprised that he had so many different ideas rushing around his head. Maybe everybody who was different was full of such thoughts, just like his mother had told him. It excited him to think that.

The school had just gone on a spring break. Dodo was about to enjoy a two-week vacation with his family. It had been a long time since he had traveled to the Rocky Mountain and seen Green River. His mother and he made plans to go to Green River with his neighbors his first weekend home.

When the weekend finally arrived, Dodo woke up early and prepared his backpack and camping stove to make lunch outdoors. Then he rushed into his mother's room to awaken her.

"It's 8 o'clock, Mom," he said. "Time to start our trip to Green River."

Tada opened her sleepy eyes "Did you already pack the food and drink?"

Dodo smiled. "Ready to go. I'm just waiting for you." Dodo could barely wait another minute.

"OK, let me get up and see."

Tada got up, cleaned the room, and was just taking some fresh cheese from the storeroom when the doorbell rang. It was Madam Jude and her son Mead, who were joining them on the trip.

"Ready to go?" Madam Jude said to Tada.

"Ready," Tada said, and the four set out.

Tada and Jude, whose backpacks were heavy with food and equipment, trudged behind the exuberant Dodo and Mead, who frolicked and laughed in the bright morning air.

Dodo and his companions crossed many miles of lush green fields to reach the Green River at the foot of the Rocky Mountains. But it seemed a short time for two young chickens who had been stuck in school for months and now were able to run and jump in the beautiful meadows along the way.

There were many strange flowers and grasses to gaze upon—red, yellow, pink and white. Butterfly and bees flitted about them, and the sweet perfume of flowers and young grass filled the air. Sunlight glittered on the fragile wings of dragonflies that hovered above. Dodo and Mead were awed by the wonderful picture. They chased the bees and butterflies across the fields, and stopped to watch a bee quietly standing on a thunder-and-lightning rose, sipping its nectar. When he was full, he spread his wings lazily and flew into the sky.

"Dodo, Mead, let's go. Green River is right over there," Tada called to the two playing children.

Dodo and Mead hurried to catch up with their mothers and were greeted by the sight of a magnificent mountain, soaring into the sky, full of lush trees and berries.

"Wow!" Dodo cried. There was a calm river at the foot of the mountains, which Dodo knew must be Green River. Elephants, zebras and cattle drank together on its banks, enjoying the coolness of the water under the hot sun.

"Dodo, Mead. Are you hungry?" Tada asked.

"A little." Dodo and Mead said at the same time.

"Let's stop and have lunch here, then." Jude suggested, picking a shady spot beneath a golden larch tree near the mountain.

"Good idea," Tada agreed, and the two women laid down their backpacks and began to unload their picnic. They laid an old tablecloth on the grass and placed the camping stove on top of it, while Dodo and Mead played nearby.

Dodo thought how nice it was to eat in such a beautiful setting—short grass, tall grass, a clear, sweet river, friendly animals and fresh air. Dodo suddenly wondered why he and the other chicken children had to spend so much time at school. Why not build a home near the river and enjoy life immersed in nature? He decided he would share this idea with his mother and Mead after lunch.

But just as the four travelers were beginning their lunch, they noticed the animals drinking from the river suddenly lift their heads and sniff the air, a sign of danger, Dodo had learned in school. Tada and Jude felt it, too.

"Put down your food and run for shelter," Tada said to the children. "Run!"

Dodo had never seen his mother so frightened. And the animals scrambled from the riverbank in all directions, filling the air with dust as they stampeded across the fields. It frightened Dodo. Whatever had scared the animals must be very dangerous to cause such havoc in so short a time.

Dodo and Mead hurried after their mothers to a nearby cave. They were afraid they might die if they didn't reach the cave fast. Apparently, Tada and Jude felt the same way. They turned and picked up their children in their beaks, then scurried into the cave.

The cave was a natural stalactite hole with water inside. Tada and Jude put Dodo and Mead on the ground, and they all took a deep breath. Dodo and Mead were shaking. Their mothers helped clean the dirt that had settled in their feathers when they ran. Then the mothers peeked outside to see what was happening.

Dodo and Mead were calmer now, and Dodo became curious about what was going on. He joined his mother and Jude at the mouth of the cave and peeked outside.

What he saw made him shudder!

An incredible animal sailed in the sky above them It had two long gray wings, a sharp beak, and strong yellow claws. Suddenly, it dove from the top of the mountain to the river like a bolt of lightning.

Dodo stared at the creature, open-mouthed, his heart beating rapidly. He couldn't believe that there was such a great flying animal on the earth. It glided on the winds like a butterfly, but a hundred times faster. Dodo wondered what the name of this amazing creature was as it lowered its claws and scooped up a fish from the deep cool water, then flew back into the sky.

Dodo's fear gave way to amazement. It was such a beautiful and perfect animal. He wanted to know everything about it.

"Mom, mom!" he cried, pointing to the magnificent creature. "What's that giant butterfly called?"

"It is not a butterfly," Tada corrected him. "It is a bird. The bald eagle." Tada pulled Dodo closer to her to keep him safe.

*Bald eagle!* Dodo thought. What a wonderful name, so strong and free. Dodo held the name in his heart.

"The bald eagle is the strongest and bravest animal in the sky," Tada continued. "He is the king of the sky. No other bird can challenge him. But he only eats small ground animals, such as wild rabbits. The bald eagle has no interest in animals like elephants and horses. Chickens, fish, and rabbits are the best food for him. You must beware of him always. His sharp eyes can see a fleeing rabbit from far atop the mountain, and he will fly down like a spark and steal that rabbit's life."

The four of them waited awhile longer. When Tada and Jude noticed the other animals returning to Green River, they left the cave. Mom and Jude took a deep breath, and searched the skies, while Mead looked about for their abandoned lunch. He hadn't finished eating and was still hungry.

"Mom, I want some more to eat," he said to Jude. "Can we go back to our picnic?"

"Sounds good to me," Jude said. "Let's finish the rest of our lunch. It is a blame and shameful thing to waste food." She looked at Tada. "Ready?" she said.

Tada nodded. "Yes, I'm ready. Are you still hungry, Dodo?" Tada she asked, looking at her boy.

"No, thanks! Mom," Dodo said, watching the sky. "I'm thirsty from running. I think I'll get a drink from the river." Dodo watched the sky, uninterested in the delectable insects he'd been so hungrily munching before the eagle appeared..

"All right. Jude, Mead and I will finish our picnic. Just please stay by the riverbank near us, and holler if you're in danger." Tada was a bit surprised that Dodo had eaten so little. Perhaps the bald eagle had frightened him more than she knew.

Meanwhile, Dodo approached the riverbank and lowered his head for a drink. There were so many large animals nearby. Elephants and zebras were washing themselves with mud to keep away the insects.

Dodo wasn't frightened, because he had been told they only eat grass and not chickens. Then he saw his reflection in the water and jumped with surprise. It was the first time he had ever seen himself. And suddenly he knew why his classmates always laughed at him. His wings were much too long and his beak much sharper than any of the other chickens', even his mom's.

After a cool, sweet drink, he doused himself with water, then lay down in the sunshine, staring into the sky. The sky was clear. Not an eagle in sight. But the memory of the bald eagle haunted him. He could almost see it again.

Dodo wasn't scared anymore, though. Rather, he admired the eagle, its ability to soar through the clouds. It must be amazing, to be so strong and free. There were no other birds like them. Land animals would never know this feeling. They had enough to do just to stay alive on the ground.

Just then a crazy idea popped into Dodo's head, making him excited and happy, and he ran back to join the others. .

"What's the matter?" Tada asked, mistaking his excitement for fear when Dodo ran up to her. Mead was still shaking after the eagle scare.

"Mom," Dodo said. "We chickens have wings and feathers just like eagles. So why can't we soar into the sky?"

Tada smiled. "Cute boy! We may have wings and feathers, but they are no longer useful to fly with. It has been a long time since chickens flew."

"Really? We could fly before?" Dodo couldn't believe his ears.

Tada nodded. "Yes. At the beginning of the early world, the great-great-grandfather of chickens could fly. He flew with the eagles, just a little more slowly.

"But then there was a huge earthquake. The chicken family had to find shelter to save themselves. Many animals suffered death and illness in that tragedy. The survivors of the chickens were lucky enough to land in a warm cave at the foot of the Rocky Mountains. For many years they lived happily on the ground, since there was an abundance of food and a warm home there. They flew less and less.

"Hundreds of years past, and because the chickens had not flown for so long, their wings became useless for flight. Soon, they could no longer soar on the winds."

"You mean, we couldn't dance in the sun with the eagles even if we wanted to?" Dodo asked, upset that the ability to fly had been given to him and taken away again so quickly.

Tada hesitated. "Well," she said at last, *"I* couldn't. But you can."

Dodo stared at her. He thought he must have misunderstood. "Did you say I can fly?" he said. "But I don't understand. "Why can I fly, but not you, Mom?"

Tada put her beak next to his ear and whispered, "Because, my Dodo, you don't belong to us."

# Chapter 3

Dodo couldn't believe his ears. It was the first time he had ever heard such a thing. He had no interest in playing with Mead anymore. He just wanted to be alone with Tada so he could ask more questions. All he could do was think about those words: "You don't belong to us."

Finally, Jude and Mead went off to play in the river, leaving Dodo and Tada alone. Dodo snuggled close to his mother and said, "Please, Tada, tell me again what you meant about me not belonging to you."

"It's true," Tada said after exhaling a deep breathe. She held Dodo tight. "You do not belong to us."

"Then who am I? Am I a chicken?" Dodo was very confused.

"No, you are not a chicken. In fact, you are the child of a bald eagle. It is a story that goes back to the time when you were a baby in the nest." Tada pulled Dodo close to her, her eyes twinkling as she remembered…

"It was summer, nine years ago, when you were born to a bald eagle in the Rocky Mountains," she began. "In order to avoid other animals' attacks, the bald eagles build their nests at the tops of the mountain cliffs and in high trees. That way, other birds and animals have a hard time reaching the eagles' nests. But the eagles still have to deal with the environment and unexpected attacks now and then. For that reason, they always lay two eggs, just in case one doesn't survive.

"You and your brother Gain were only three days old when I first met you. I went out for food and medicinal grasses one hot summer afternoon for Mead. After several days nesting, your parents were very hungry, so your father flew away, searching for food. Your mother was in charge of looking after you and Gain.

"Because you and Gain were hungry, too, you began to fight with one another. Your mother went out to find your father to help her. She didn't know you would soon be fighting to the death.

"It is natural for baby eagles to fight with each other. But your older brother Gain was much more aggressive than you, since he was stronger. All you could do was try to avoid Gain's attack.

"Gain never considered that you were his baby brother and that he should look after you. He just kept attacking, trying to eat you. Baby eagles can't live without lots of food, and it seemed as if your parents would never return to feed you. The only way Gain thought he could live was by eating you! He was born with this instinct, and soon you were bleeding profusely from his attack. You were very weak, and soon would die.

11

"Meanwhile, I was searching for a medicinal plant for Mead. He had caught a cold shortly after he was born, and nothing our chicken family did to help him had cured him. Jude was very weak after nesting Mead's egg for so long, so I offered to help her and find the medicine.

"The particular medicinal plant I was looking for to cure Mead's illness is very difficult to find. A wise chicken taught us that we could find valuable plants at the top of the Rocky Mountains. Now, Jude had warned me never go to the top of the mountain because it is very dangerous. The bald eagle and other mountain dwellers would attack me if they came across me on the road.

"But Jude is a kind and warm-hearted chicken. I could not let her son die. So I risked climbing the steep mountain to find the medicine she needed.

"It was sorely hot that day. Uncle Sun was angry and sent down more heat than usual. Many of the chickens and other animals stayed in caves or under trees to keep cool. They would wait for the coming of evening to hunt. Therefore, I didn't need to worry about meeting any wolves or other predators on the way to the mountaintop.

"But without any cool winds, it was very hot in the mountains. The higher I climbed, the hotter I felt. Soon, I was so tired and thirsty that I had to rest every few steps.

"I unloaded the basket on my back, and fanned myself with my wings. While I was cooling off, I was able to enjoy the beauty of the Rocky Mountains up close.

"I had only seen the mountain from a distance before this, and it was quite different from the way it is now. It was not bald as you see it today. There were some different plants whose names I don't know. Of course, you need to be careful of some plants, because they are poisonous. But I didn't learn which ones at school. The only plant I knew was the one that would cure Mead.

"That plant, I was told, had two short leaves and four round leaves on one stem. It was bright green and there was only one in any clump of plants that would help me. I would find the same plant every few feet, some of the older chickens had taught me, but the way you recognized the core plant that would save Mead was that all six leaves rose in different directions to the sky.

"After my rest, I felt a little better, and continued my search. I had to hurry and find the medicine for Jude so that I could reach home before the sunset. Once the sun set, not only would I have a hard time finding my way home, but the wolves would come out to hunt for their supper.

"If I couldn't find that grass in time, my life would be in danger, and Mead was dying. The plant I was looking for was his last hope. I had to keep myself alive and get the medicine to Mead as quickly as possible. I hadn't planned on what I would do if I couldn't find the grass before sunset, or if I should run across a pack of wolves or other predatory animals on the way home. I only thought about saving Mead's life. If I failed, Jude would lose her lovely baby, and that would be terrible.

"Uncle Sun continued to beat down upon the earth, and although his heat sapped my energy, I never lost hope. All I could think of was how to find Mead's medicine so I could go home.

"Finally, heaven decided to help Jude and me. At the top of the mountain, near the nest of the bald eagle, I found the plant I was looking for. The first plant I saw looked like the right plant, but the two short and four round leaves were all facing in the same direction. Only the core plant would have leaves that pointed in six different directions. Old chickens in the family had told us to never use this plant if there wasn't a core plant. Without a core plant, the others were poison. Any animal that touched them would die instantly.

"The eagles had nested nearby as protection against attacking animals. You couldn't gain access to their nest without touching the plant and dying. I had to watch my steps carefully to search for the core grass.

"At last, I found it near the nest of the bald eagle. Two short leaves and four round leaves. All six leaves were pointing in different directions toward the sky. I was very excited about my discovery and jumped for joy, because now Mead would recover. Jude would be thrilled to see her lovely baby smiling again.

"I knew I needed to gather the medicinal plant quickly, before any of the adult eagles came back to the nest. Luckily, I was able to pick those lifesaving plants before they returned.

"Wise chickens had warned me that eagles had very sharp instincts when it came to anyone approaching their nest. They would fly back to protect their baby eagles from thousands of miles away in no time.

"Maybe that's the power of love. Love shines through time and distance. Although the eagle is the cruelest of birds, they are very kind to their children, as we are to ours." She smiled at Dodo, then continued, "I only wanted to pick up enough of the medicinal plant as I needed and leave that place as soon as possible, before the adult eagles returned. So I picked the plants as fast as I could and put them into my basket. The plants didn't have deep roots, so it was easy to fill the basket in a very short time.

"As I worked, I noticed a lot of noise coming from the nest—the cries of baby eagles. It frightened me. I could see they were very small baby eagles. Their eyes weren't even open yet. They were too weak and small to hurt me. But their noise would attract their parents, it being a signal of danger.

"I stopped working for a moment, and turned to the nest. Maybe I could figure out what was wrong and stop the baby eagles from crying out

When I approached the nest, Gain, your old brother, was attacking you, although you were badly hurt already. I had heard that baby eagles will kill their siblings so they can get all the food, but it was the first time I'd ever seen it happen.

"If the mother eagle was there, she would stop Gain. But she wasn't. I thought it was too late to save you. And even if I could, the eagles would follow the scent I left on the nest and kill me if I touched any of their babies, even if I didn't hurt them.

So I could only stand there and watch the horrible scene of Gain attacking you. There was blood all over you—on your wings and shoulders, and you were shivering. You didn't know that death was upon you.

"You tried to escape Gain's sharp beak, backing away to the edge of the nest. But you went too far, and suddenly you were falling. The nest was built on a cliff, and you couldn't fly. You would be killed falling from such heights.

"Shortly after you fell, Gain succumbed to the heat and lack of food, and died. It was very sad watching those two babies fight for their lives. But it is nature's way of teaching eagles to survive and to be brave in the face of death, so that they can fly freely and mightily in the heavens.

"I wished, at that moment, that I could fly. Then I recalled what a dangerous situation I was in. The parent eagles would be back any minute, and they would assume that I killed their babies. They would never believe that I hadn't laid a finger on their children.

"My heart racing with fear, I picked up my basket and ran away."

# Chapter 4

Tada took a long drink from a canteen of water, her gaze moving from the Rocky Mountains to Jude and Mead splashing in the shallow water on the banks of Green River. Her eyes returned to Dodo, and she gave him a warm hug.

"I ran like the wind, because the bald eagle would be back any second. It would a terrible misfortune if we should meet. So I picked up my bag, held it tightly, and searched for the right path down the mountain.

"Uncle Sun had disappeared behind a cloud, tired after a long afternoon. I knew he would return home within hours, and that I needed to leave the mountain before it grew too dark.

"I could not see the beauty of my surroundings because of the fear that gripped me. I sensed the bald eagle was coming. He and his wife were flying great distances, and they were angry. They believed that their babies were being attacked by a small animal. All they could think about was catching and punishing the culprit.

"I almost lost my way on the mountain. Bushes and brambles tore at my feathers as I scrambled to find my way, but I couldn't stop. *Run, run, run away* was all I could think about. The quicker I got off the mountain, the safer I would feel.

"Finally, I reached the foot of the mountain, and I stopped to catch my breath. I glanced back at the mountain. I was safe now. Even though I had heard the wolves cry from deep in the mountains, I knew they were busy hunting other animals. So I decided to rest a while before returning home.

"But just as I was about to sit down on a nearby rock to rest, something horrific caught my sight in the nearby field. There was something moving in the grass. I was immediately on my guard. I hoped it would turn out to be nothing more than some insects flitting through the weeds.

"Part of me thought I should run, but part of me was curious as well. What was it that was moving in the grass? I didn't sense danger, which I believed I would if it was anything that could threaten my life. And maybe it was some tasty locusts that I could bring home for supper. So I decided to move closer and see what was rustling the grass.

" 'What is this?' I asked myself when I got closer. It was not tasty locusts that rustled the grass at all, but rather, the baby eagle that had dropped from its nest. He was shivering, and his bleeding wounds had turned the grass red. But I could see him breathing and knew he was still alive.

"That baby eagle was you," Tada said, smoothing Dodo's feathers. "You were alive, even after falling from the top of the Rocky Mountains. It was a miracle! I marveled at your will to live.

"But you were bleeding so profusely, I knew you would die if you didn't receive treatment soon. Your parents would be arriving at the nest soon, but how long would it take for them to find you at the foot of the mountain? You might very well be dead when they found you. What should I do?

"I decided that I couldn't leave you there. I would take you home and nurse you back to health. I would bring you back to your parents when you were better. I picked up your weak body, placed it carefully in my basket, and hurried home. When I came to Jude's house, Mead still had a high fever. I gave Jude the medicine I'd found. She started to cry. 'Tada, Mead would die if it wasn't for you. You are his savior. How can I thank you?'

" 'Your happiness is thanks enough,' I told her. Then, hearing you whimper in the basket, I asked, 'Where is the doctor?'

"'In the living room. Is something the matter with you?' she asked"

" 'No, no. I'm OK,'" I assured her. 'I'll talk to you later.' Then I rushed into the living room to find the doctor.

"The doctor examined you and gave me some medicine. 'He will be fine in a week,' he assured me.

"I took you home and nursed you day after day, waiting for the day when you would be well enough to return to your family.

"Six days later, you were fully recovered from your wounds. I wrapped you in warm blankets inside my basket and started the dangerous journey back to the mountains. But when I got there, the nest was gone. I thought perhaps I had made a mistake, and decided to come back tomorrow, when I had rested and could search again. But the nest was not there the next day, either.

"Maybe your parents thought that Gain had eaten you, and they abandoned that sad place. I tried to find your parents several times after that, but with always the same result. I finally gave up looking and decided to raise you myself."

Dodo stared at his mother in astonishment. He was the son of an eagle. It was hard to believe that this was really happening.

"My child," Tada said. "I didn't want to tell you truth. I love you so much, I was afraid I would lose you if you knew. But the truth must always come out. You are the child of an eagle. Now you understand why you are different from the other chickens in the way you look and think. Although you never learned to fly, you are always an eagle no matter what."

Dodo recalled the beauty of the soaring eagle he had just seen. "Will I be able to fly someday?" he asked.

"It is possible," Tada replied. "But only if you truly desire it. You see, it is not easy as it seems. You must give up your life with me and the other chickens and become a true eagle. You must rid yourself of every habit and way you have learned until now. You will not be a chicken any more. Change your mind, change your life, and you will learn to fly."

Dodo's head spun. So much was happening so fast. He was an eagle, but in order to fulfill his destiny—his dream—he would have to leave his dear mother. He didn't want to leave his mother yet. But the image of that soaring eagle stayed in his mind. He didn't know what to do.

"My dear," his mother said, noticing his agitation. "You don't need to make a decision now. You can think about what you want to do. Learning to fly is not something you decide to do in one day." Tada smiled at her cute baby.

Tada's words made Dodo feel better. He would have time to think about what he wished for in his life. His mother hadn't given him a time limit to make his decision. But in his heart, Dodo knew he must start growing up now.

\* \* \*

Time passed. Dodo returned to school after a great spring holiday. Hera, the president of the chicken school, announced he would choose the best of his followers to take over his position when he died. That meant the chosen chicken would become the leader of all the chickens and lead them into the future.

Everyone knew that Dodo and Bipa were the first choices to become the new leader, because they were excellent in everything they did. Bipa studied constantly, waiting for Hera to make the announcement. Although he was cruel to his friends sometimes, he was a hard worker.

But Dodo seemed not to be interested in becoming the chosen one. He daydreamed all the time, staring out the window at the blue sky in the autumn morning. Although it was cool, now, the shining sun and blue sky reminded him of another time.

The more he looked, the more he thought of the bald eagle, soaring across the sky. The words of Tada rang in his heart. "You can fly like an eagle. You *are* an eagle." The blue sky and white clouds and freedom made him happy. He thought the bald eagle must be happy to fly so high because they felt the way he did—brave, strong and free. There were no limits for them. They owned the sky. He smiled to himself.

"Excuse me, Dodo, could you please tell the answer to this math question?" Neid, his math teacher asked, noticing him daydreaming.

"Sorry," Dodo said, pulling himself out of his daydream and back into the classroom.

"You must pay attention if you want to become the successor to Hera," Neid told him. "You must work hard for that position. It upsets me that you do not pay attention." Neid threw down her book and left the class in a huff.

"Ha, Dodo. The game isn't over." Bipa said when Neid was gone. "Better quit your daydreaming." But Dodo could see that Bipa was glad this had happened, because Neid would be a key judge in the final election.

Dodo ignored Bipa and went out for a breath of air. Mead followed him out, wondering why Dodo hadn't gotten angry with Bipa. In the past, Dodo would have fought him for what he said.

"What's the matter with you?" Mead asked Dodo.

Dodo turned around and, seeing it was Mead said, "Nothing. I'm OK." He sighed. "Mead, I want to fly into the heavens."

Mead's mouth dropped open. "Are you crazy? Chickens can't fly. Not even Hera."

"But I am not a chicken," Dodo said, deciding to tell Mead the truth. "Mom said I was born an eagle."

"What? An eagle?" Mead could hardly believe what he was hearing. "OK, so maybe you don't want to become Hera's successor. And suppose that you are an eagle and can fly. You will have to leave all of us and your mother to live like an eagle. Won't you miss us? You will lose everything you have, and you don't even know if you can achieve your dream of flying after living with the chickens these many years. You have become a chicken. Have you ever seen an eagle walk like you or eat like you?"

Dodo raised his head to the blue sky and considered Mead's words. Mead didn't believe he would pursue such a crazy dream.

Just then, Hera came toward them. "Dodo, are you OK?" he asked. Mead knew that Hera probably wanted to tell Dodo something important about the election, so he left.

When Mead was gone, Hera continued, "Dodo, I know you have worked very hard and want to become our leader. Please don't let Neid's words defeat you. I think you will be the best leader we've ever had. You can definitely win the election."

Dodo wanted to tell Hera about being an eagle and flying, but he stopped when he saw how pleased Hera was that Dodo might be the next leader. It made Dodo wonder about his future. On the one hand, he could be the leader of all the chickens. On the other, he was an eagle, and he wanted to fly like an eagle.

It was time to talk to his mom and see if she could help him figure it out.

# **Chapter 5**

When Dodo got home, he found his mother in the kitchen, washing the dishes. "Mom," he said, "I'm confused about my future."

"My dear," Tada said, wiping her hands on her apron and sitting down at the table. "Don't worry about your confusion. It is natural to go back and forth about what you want. Tell me, what are you considering doing now with your life?" Tada smiled kindly at her baby, and poured him a cup of orange juice from a pitcher on the table.

Dodo, seated beside her, drank his juice, then, gathering his courage he said, "As you know, there will be a game to select the successor to the next leader in the chicken family. President Hera likes me very much and hopes I can win the game. But I also remember what you told me on the banks of the Green River. My best friend Mead warned me to forget my wild dream and concentrate on the election game. He thinks I would give up many valuable things if I pursue my crazy dream. I don't know whether I could win the game or not. Now I feel like a stranger standing on the corner of a crossroad. Which way I should go?"

Tada smiled, nodding her head. "You are at a crossroad. That is something to celebrate. It means you have two choices to pursue. Either way will take you on a different magical and amazing adventure."

"But how do I know if I make the right decision? Is it all just a gamble?"

Tada thought for a moment. "The truth is, we don't know where the future lies. What will happen? We cannot predict the future, but we can take control of the present. There are always friends, parents, and neighbors to help you decide what you want for your future.

"They'll try to help you make a good choice. But all of them, including you, forget one important key. Any advice and suggestions they give you are from their point of view instead of yours. You are the master of your fate. It is your life. You may listen to everybody's advice and suggestions, but your are the final decision-maker."

"But I'm afraid I might make a mistake." Dodo said, wanting to be both the chicken leader and an eagle.

"Be brave," his mother told him. "Your fear is only a worry about something in the future that hasn't happened. Don't worry, but look at both of your desires seriously, because once you make a commitment, you can't turn back. Overcome your fear and you will be relieved and happy with the results."

"But what should I do?" Dodo said, wanting his mother to give him the answer.

"My child, you know in your heart what you want to do. Be brave and say it aloud. Don't keep your decision hidden in your heart. It is very simple to make a right choice. No matter what others say, right or wrong, set their words aside. You have only one choice to make. You will find that you will never be upset about your choice when you follow your heart. Listen to your heart and go for your dream. I'll never tell you what to do with your life."

Dodo took a deep breath. "Mom, I think I know what I want to do." He stopped for a moment, then said, "I want to fly."

"That's wonderful!" his mother said. "I am very glad to hear that. You have decided your future." Tada patted Dodo's head softly. "Now rest for today. Tomorrow you will start searching for your dream."

With that, Tada went back to cleaning her dishes.

* * *

The next day, Tada woke up her sleeping Dodo to ready him for his journey. Dodo opened his eyes to the brightest day of the whole week. It was an auspicious sign to start his dream journey.

After breakfast, Jude and Mead brought many sacks of corn from the warehouse, where Tada had stored it. Tada thanked her kind neighbor. Dodo glanced about his room one last time, then took the corn and other provisions, and left the house with Tada.

"Dodo, did you decide not to attend today's competition?" Mead asked, upset that Dodo would leave them for such a long time.

Dodo had almost forgotten about the game. Today was the final game before the election.

Mead noticed a change come over Dodo, as if he wasn't sure if he should leave now. Mead was happy to see it. "Mother," he said, "the final competition will be happening soon. We don't want to miss it" Mead hoped this would make Dodo want to stay and play in the competition after all.

"We must wait and see Dodo off. He's your best friend," Jude said, not understanding what Mead was trying to do.

"Mother and Madam Tada," Mead said to the two mothers, "the competition is held on the way to the Rocky Mountains. We could stay at the game for a while, and that way Dodo would get a rest on his long journey." Mead was very happy about this idea, thinking he could get Dodo to stay with them after that.

Tada felt awkward, not sure how Dodo would take this. "Dodo, what do you think?" she said. "Can we watch the game before going to the mountain?"

"Sure," Dodo said, but his mind seemed to be very far away.

The game was held on the playground between the school and Green River. All the students and their parents had come to see the exciting game. Dodo had never seen so many chickens together at one time.

The chickens made a circle around the playground, and the players stood in rows in the center, waiting for the game to begin. The referee stood in the middle of the circle, and Hera sat in a place of honor with his wife. They were watching the game carefully, trying to decide who would be his successor next year. All the chicken children and students cheered for their friends in the competition, hoping they would win. Bipa did warm up exercises. It seemed he still didn't know that Dodo wouldn't be competing today.

"Dodo, maybe they're worrying about whether you can get to your place in line on time." Mead pointed to some of his friends in the north corner of the playground.

"I know," Dodo replied, feeling a little sorry that he wouldn't be able to say goodbye to his friends and teachers before he left. "Please thank them for me, and tell them where I went after I leave."

It was for the best that he didn't say good-bye in person, Dodo knew. They might not understand why he had to pursue his dream to fly, and they might even convince him to change his mind.

"You do know this means Bipa will win the final game, don't you?" Mead said, hoping to convince Dodo to stay.

"Maybe," Dodo replied. "But I don't care about that any more. Besides, Bipa will be a good leader if Hera teaches him for a year. He always tried to beat me at everything we did." Dodo searched his friend's eyes. "Mead, we're still friends, right?"

"Yes," Mead said.

"Then please be happy and proud of my choice."

Mead took a deep breath. "No matter what happens, Dodo, we are always friends. Even if you become a bald eagle."

"I'll fly to see you when I learn how. And I truly believe I can learn to fly."

"I believe you can, too, since you're giving up so much to pursue your dream. Your courage makes me proud."

Dodo smiled. "Thank you, Mead. You're a good friend. Let's go, OK?" Dodo looked around one last time before leaving the playground.

Tada and Jude, who had been lounging nearby, were ready to go, too.

* * *

The four of them were happy on the way to Green River. The woods and fields were beautiful in the autumn morning. The grass was very green, waving pleasantly in the warm wind. Uncle Sun, who had lost his summer heat, smiled lazily at the ground.

Soon Green River and the Rocky Mountains were before them. A few animals drank at the river, while others searched for food for the coming winter.

"Dodo, are you tired?" Tada asked. "We could rest a moment if you want to lay your backpack down for a bit." Tada shook her wings and touched the sweat on Dodo's forehead.

"OK," Dodo replied. "I could use a rest. We can rest on the banks of the river."

Jude, Mead, Dodo, and Tada went down to the river. Dodo and Mead scooped water into some cups for their moms. Then they pulled out the corn they'd brought for lunch.

"Mom," Dodo said as he ate his lunch. "I think you should go home after we finish eating. I need to find that nest by myself." Dodo must have thought a thousand times about his birth nest after learning he was born an eagle.

"Yes, I suppose you're right," Tada admitted reluctantly. "You must find your birth place by yourself." Tears came to Tada's eyes, but she dared not let Dodo see. She quickly wiped them away and said, "I'm sorry I'm not able to teach you to fly, my child. I hope you will achieve your dream someday."

Dodo smiled gratefully. He knew it would be a long time before he learned to fly and could see her again, and he appreciated the support she gave him.

"Listen to me," Tada continued. "Hold on to your dream and never give up. If you trust and believe it faithfully, without question, you will make it no matter what difficulties you may encounter. Trust yourself and your natural flying ability. If you hope for something deep in your heart, heaven will open the gates of opportunity and help your achieve it. We are very proud of your courage and brave heart. Always remember that we will be on your side no matter what happens in the future, whether in good or bad times."

Dodo nodded. "I'll remember," he said.

"You can take the rest of the corn to your nest. There is enough there for the whole year, in case you don't have time to hunt."

Dodo knew it took Tada a whole week to forage that corn for him. His eyes filled with tears and he couldn't speak.

"Don't you worry about your mother," Tada said. "I'll have dinner with Jude and Mead. They'll be happy to put out an extra plate for me."

Then she pulled something out from beneath her wings and held it out to Dodo. It was a bright green stone on a purple ribbon. The stone sparkled in the sunshine. "This is magic stone," she told Dodo. "You will learn to speak the eagle's language and think like an eagle before you finally learn to fly. This stone will help you. Hold it in your beak, and you will understand the words of eagles and speak to them freely."

"The purple ribbon belongs to you. It was with you when you dropped from the nest. Keep it with you always. When you finally learn to fly, tie that ribbon around your claws and we will know that is you, my son, Dodo." Tada placed the ribbon in Dodo's claws.

"I'll make you proud of me, Mom. I promise," Dodo said.

"I know you will," Tada said. "But one last thing before I go. If you ever decide that you won't be able to fly, please come back to us. No matter whether you make it or not, we will welcome you home."

"I'll learn as fast as I can and fly to see you," Dodo promised. Then, tears filling his eyes, he hugged his dear mother. When he looked at Mead and Jude, they had tears in their eyes as well.

"OK, Dodo," Tada said, wiping her eyes. "Be brave now." Then she placed the sacks of corn on his shoulder.

"Thank you for coming to see me off," Dodo said, hugging Jude and Mead warmly.

"Be good, child." Jude said sadly, knowing Dodo would soon disappear deep into the mountains.

Dodo nodded, then turned to his friend. "Thank you for being my friend, Mead," he said. "Please take care of my mom. And please promise you'll find me if anything serious happens to her."

"I will, buddy," Mead said, giving him a hug.

Dodo turned to look at his mother and friends one last time. Then he picked up the magic stone in his beak and started the journey to find his dream.

# Chapter 6

Carrying his supply of corn, Dodo continued his journey. He knew that eagles like to build nests at the top of high trees or on mountain cliffs, and thought maybe he could find an empty nest to sleep in. Otherwise, he would have to find branches and build his own.

He was hoping to find a nest before sunset. It would be best to find his birth nest. Not only would he feel better to stay in the place where he was born, but maybe his parents would return there someday.

He had a long way to go, but he was thrilled to be starting his amazing adventure. He smiled at the blue sky and sunshine, and began to climb the road to the Rocky Mountains.

Although he had never climbed this mountain before, Dodo recognized many things on his way to the top. Perhaps it was recalling a thousand times Tada's story about saving his life. He had always thought that the Rocky Mountains were made of bare rock, but he was totally wrong. Green grasses, beautiful colorful flowers, and air fresher than he had ever smelled greeted him on his way. Locusts and other insects flitted in the sunshine. It was more beautiful than he had ever imagined. It added to Dodo's excitement as he hopped along the road to the mountain's peak.

After a while, Dodo began to feel a little tired, so he dropped his sack full of corn and sat down in a patch of grass to take a rest. There were some little yellow flowers nearby smiling at his sweating face. Dodo picked one and placed it in the feathers at the top of his head. He sang a simple song he had learned in class and took deep breaths of the sweet air wafting from the mountain grass. As he relaxed, he thought to himself, *Carrying around two heavy sacks of corn is really slowing me down. Why don't I leave one of the sacks of corn buried here and come back after I find a nest?*

He found an undisturbed spot of ground near a bush, and dug a deep hole in the dry earth. Then he placed one of the sacks of corn inside, buried it, and camouflaged it all with some leaves. After scratching a mark in the dirt so he would remember where he buried it, he wiped the sweat from his face, pleased at himself and his clever idea. Then, slinging the remaining sack over his shoulder, he began to climb the mountain again.

Along the way, Dodo picked up a branch here and there. They would be good for building a nest. Branches are very abundant in the mountain forests, but only short, pliable ones make a comfortable nest. But Dodo's eyesight was very sharp, so it wasn't hard for him to find the right branches.

The sun sparkled on the lush vegetation that covered the mountain. It was a good time to explore. The insects would be returning home for dinner and sleep soon. The whole area had become calmer and more silent, the only with sound the footsteps and labored breathing of a little bird searching for his nest.

Suddenly, Dodo noticed some flowers with their leaves pointing toward the sky in six different directions. Although he had never seen the flowers before, they seemed very familiar to him. He searched his memory, trying to figure out why.

Then it came to him. This was the plant Tada had told him about picking when he was just a baby still in his nest. These were the leaves that saved Mead's life. Better still, his mom had mentioned that the leaves were near the place where she first caught sight of an eagle's nest and two baby eagles.

He raised his head and discovered a nest in the branches of a tree, overhanging a cliff. The tree was growing from a lower ledge, so Dodo was able to walk to the nest. When he reached it, he saw that it was still clean and sound after these many years. Strong rain and winds had kept it that way, almost like new.

Dodo stood in the middle of the nest where he was born, and a strange feeling of excitement came over him. The mountain seemed to spin, and it was as if he had already learned to fly and soar on the winds. He imagined himself crossing seas and mountains, and finding his real parents. It was all wonderful and nothing could stop him. Dodo jumped for joy, and cried out in happiness deep from within his heart.

He calmed down after a bit. The corn sack had been abandoned several feet away. If he wanted to eat tonight, he had better retrieve it. He was getting pretty hungry. If he was home, he would be leaving school right now, hurrying home for dinner. Tada would be waiting for him with a table full of delicious food. There was always a candle in the window to light his way home. Recalling that, Dodo was determined to learn to fly as soon as he could, so he could return home to see his mother.

But after his long journey and hard work, the corn tasted delicious, and Dodo ate it gratefully. His mother had sorted the corn into many small bags inside the large sack so Dodo would know exactly how much to eat. Dodo smiled to himself, thinking how wonderful it was to have someone like Tada to love him. He decided that this was the most delicious food he ever tasted.

After dinner, he patted his full stomach and nestled down in the nest for a good night's sleep beneath the sparkling sky. There were so many, many stars blinking at him in the darkness. To the north was a moon boat. It was such a beautiful night. Dodo had always watched TV or done homework after dinner before this. He never knew the deep beauty of the night that he had been missing.

And the stars, oh the stars reminded Dodo of his future with their sparkling light. In his mind's eye he saw a brave and strong eagle spreading his long wings and soaring on the winds in the blue sky. There were green fields below, and farmers planting maize. The waterfall in front of the mountains was like a satin ribbon from heaven. A flock of wild geese flew below him, heading south for the winter.

Dodo's wings grew lighter and lighter. He felt like he was back in his bed at home, with the smiling moon lulling him to sleep. Pulling some branches over himself for warmth, he fell into a deep sleep.

* * *

The next morning, Dodo was awakened by the singing of hundreds of little birds. He kneaded his sleeping eyes and stretched to the sky. Then he took a deep breath, cleaned his nest, and stepped out for his morning exercise, on this, his first day as an eagle in the Rocky Mountains.

Uncle Sun has already taken breakfast and been up and about for over an hour. Dodo wandered around the road near his nest, just as if he were at home. Some insects had come out of their holes to start a new day, joining the birds high in the trees. But there was one bird Dodo didn't see... The bald eagle! Dodo didn't notice any bald eagles in the mountains or sky at all. He had been planning to watch how they flew and used their wings to glide through the vast blue sky. The more he studied them, he reasoned, the faster he would learn to fly. But there wasn't an eagle in sight.

Still, he didn't change his mind after eating breakfast. He was happy about his choice. He had already enjoyed many beautiful flowers, grasses, and birds in the mountains that he never had the opportunity to see before. Better yet, he didn't have to sit in class and listen to borings lessons about drawing a damn picture.

He was past all that. The whole sky would belong to him once he learned to fly. It would be an experience beyond words. His heart was filled with excitement.

So now the question was how to fly. Tada always told him to trust the sky when he had difficulties and questions in life. Why not ask him for help now?

"Blue sky," Dodo said, bowing his head, "could you tell me how to learn to fly, or show me a sign so that I may master the great skill I should have learned as a young bird?" Dodo raised his head and looked to the sky.

To his surprise, a swallow flew into sight. It flew very lightly. He watched it's wings flutter without stopping. It flew to its house with a piece of branch in its mouth, and something came clearly to Dodo's mind.

"Oh, I get it!" he exclaimed. "I don't need to watch the eagles to learn how to fly. If I study the small birds, I can learn the secrets of flying. Mom always said to me that I should change my thinking and model my behavior on the flying birds so I can totally master their ability. Think like an eagle and you will master the sky!"

Dodo was very happy about this revelation and smiled at the heavens. After realizing what he needed to do, he watched the swallows more carefully as they tried to make their way in the winds.

At least he didn't have to worry about starving while he was learning to fly. His mother had prepared a year's worth of food for him. That meant he could concentrate on learning to fly without searching for food everyday. He could focus all his energy on realizing his dream.

He watched the swallows a while longer. When they flew away to find their lunch, Dodo returned to the nest for a rest.

This went on for a week. Dodo exercised every day and looked for swallows or sparrows to study. Or sometimes he would picture them flying in his mind.

Just what was the difference between chickens and eagles? They both had feathers, and claws, and beaks, but they were so different.

Chickens were good at walking and never used their wings except to fight with their enemies. But eagles had strong, thick wings that supported them so they could fly across mountains and seas.

Chickens' mouths were made to peck at little insects in the dirt. But eagles had sharp beaks to grab the throats of fleeing rabbits and other small animals.

Chickens used their claws to dig the earth, searching for borrowing ants. But eagles used their claws to catch fish in the river and rabbits scurrying through the grass.

Chickens had average eyesight during the daytime. It was very difficult for them to see far, even to hunt their prey. But eagles were able to see their prey on earth and in the water from great distances in the sky.

But the biggest difference between chickens and eagles had to do with another kind of vision. Chickens were content to live on the earth. They had no desire to fly. But eagles lived to fly. Eagles were the masters of the sky! Nothing could stop an eagle from soaring through the clouds. Theirs was the joy of gliding on air, the happiness of being a bald eagle.

These thoughts excited Dodo. He wanted to fly immediately. But first he must master the movements of the eagle.

A wolf's cry from deep in the mountains reminded him that it was dinnertime. He hopped to his nest, ready for a big dinner because he had made such great progress and discoveries today.

He opened the sack of corn and picked some crisp kernels, then drank water from a cup made of a green leaves. It was so delicious! Dodo couldn't wait to eat more.

He opened his mouth, ready to gobble down some more corn, when suddenly a huge bird, its eyes glinting with anger, soared down toward the nest from high above, its sharp claws aiming for Dodo's throat.

# **Chapter 7**

*Run, run away!* Dodo thought in a panic. He dropped the corn he was about to eat and ran from the nest at full speed. He believed the bird would kill him without question. And Dodo was sure that he couldn't fight it.

But it was too late. The sharp claws had already ripped into Dodo's body. The huge strong wings beat Dodo's shoulders. Dodo had never experienced anything so terrible before. He had fought with Bipa and some of the other chickens before, but they always used their beaks to rip the others' feathers or neck to win a battle. Dodo was terrified by the great bird that now attacked him. He could do nothing but shiver and suffer the heavy beating.

Blood poured out off Dodo's wings. But the bird wasn't through. It lifted its huge wings again and beat Dodo some more, forcing him to the edge of the cliff.

Suddenly, Dodo forgot the pain and blood. He was falling—falling from the cliff at full speed. He tried to catch some trees branches growing from the cliff to save his life. He couldn't. He was diving headfirst toward the ground. If only he could fly!

Desperate, he lifted his strong wings and flapped them heavily. He tried his best to fly like the eagles or swallows he had seen. But he couldn't. He continued to fall straight down toward the rocks below.

Dodo lost all hope. He thought of his mother, and how sorry he was that he would die without ever learning to fly. He was always safe when his mother was with him. Nothing could attack him when she was near. Tada would always stand in front of him, shielding him from danger.

Warm tears filled his eyes, and he cried out, "Good-bye, Mom! I love you!"

The bird who had beaten him was resting in the nest, when it heard Dodo's words echo through the mountains. It stretched its head over the cliff, surprised to see that instead of flying, Dodo was plummeting to the ground. The bird spread its great wings and dove from the nest toward Dodo.

Dodo closed his eyes, waiting for the impact that would kill him, when suddenly he felt strong claws clutching him and carrying him into the sky. He stopped crying as he rose into the air, wondering whether it was the sky giving him back his life. But it didn't matter. For the first time in his life he was soaring through the clouds. It was just like flying.

The huge bird carried Dodo back to the nest and laid him gently down on the clean branches "Who are you?" the bird demanded. "Why on earth you do you speak the language of chickens?"

Dodo raised his eyes to the great creature. The bird moved its beak and spoke something into his ears, but Dodo didn't understand the words. He shook his head at the unknown bird.

"W-h-o a-r-e y-o-u?" the bird asked again, speaking slowly this time, believing Dodo didn't understand because he was so frightened. "Why didn't you fly when you started to fall?"

Dodo couldn't understand that either. The great bird couldn't speak the chicken language, while Dodo didn't know the great bird's language.

But wait! Dodo recalled the green stone his mother had given him before they parted. She said it was a magic stone that could help him understand the eagles' language. He pulled the stone from deep under his wings and placed it in his beak.

"Who on earth are you? I'll throw you down the mountain again if you don't answer me," the huge bird warned, angry at Dodo's refusal to respond. It spreads its strong wings and prepared to carry out his threat.

"No, no, no," Dodo cried. "I am an eagle. A bald eagle." The words rushed from Dodo's mouth in the other bird's language, although before this he had no idea how to speak it.

"Of course. I can see you are an eagle. So why didn't you fly when I beat you down the mountain? You'll die if you continue to play that falling game. And another thing—how do you speak the chicken language?"

It spread its wings, confused about what Dodo was doing.

"My name is Dodo. I lived with a chicken family from the time I was young, which is why I speak their language."

Dodo told the bird the whole story. The bird listened carefully, its face changing from angry to surprised, and then to embarrassed.

"I'm so sorry, Dodo. I didn't understand why you wouldn't answer me. You see, the nest you were sleeping in belongs to me. I always eat and rest here when I am tired. I flew by today and saw you eating corn in my nest. I thought you had grabbed the nest and stolen my stored food. That is why I beat you so fiercely. I'm sorry for that."

"Then why did you save my life?" Dodo asked, surprised.

"When you spoke in the chickens' language, I realized something amazing had happened that allowed you to speak that foreign language. I wanted to know how you learned it. Then, to my surprised, I saw that you couldn't fly at all, so I figured I better save you if I ever wanted to get an answer. I'm sorry I hurt you." The bird gently touched Dodo's wounds with its wings.

31

Dodo experienced a little pain when the lovely creature touched his wounds, but he said, "That's all right. I didn't thank you for saving my life, so now I thank you."

"You're very welcome. My name is Christine. Let me help you." With that, she smeared some saliva from her beak on Dodo's wounds.

"So you're a girl eagle?"

Christine didn't answer Dodo. She wiped away the blood on his feathers and worked on stopping his wounds.

While she was fixing his cuts, Dodo was able to really look at her. She was very beautiful, with strong wings and bright eyes. Her feathers were vibrant and arranged in a beautiful pattern. Her eyes were full of compassion. It was the first time Dodo had ever seen a bald eagle this close up.

"You'll be well in a couple of days," Christine assured him when she was finished. "You weren't badly hurt because you are very strong."

"Thank you for your kindness," Dodo replied. Then, a little embarrassed, he said, "You've helped me so much already, but I wonder if I could ask you, when I'm completely well, could you teach me how to fly?"

Christine smiled. "I'd be happy to," she said. Then a puzzled look came over her face. "The thing is, I never taught anyone how to fly before. I'm not sure I know how."

"Oh," Dodo dropped his head in disappointment.

"Hey," Christina said, touching his chin with her wing. "Don't give up. Tonight, I'll ask my parents how they teach little eagles to fly, and then I can show you tomorrow."

Dodo beamed.

"But you have to rest and get well first."

"You bet!" Dodo said, so excited that he was going to learn how to fly from a real eagle that he almost jumped for joy.

Christina hopped to the edge of the nest. "I have to fly back home now, or my parents will worry about me. They don't know I come here to play. This is my secret heaven. I never told them." She spread her great wings. "See you tomorrow," she called, then she flew away into the blue sky and was soon gone from Dodo's sight.

*Soon I'll be able to fly high, just like her,* Dodo thought. He could hardly wait.

\* \* \*

In the following weeks, Christine often flew to Dodo's nest. Her parents showed her many ways to teach flying. But the lessons they gave her were for teaching baby eagles. It was quite different for Dodo, because his wings were so large already. So Christine made Dodo practice flapping his wings everyday so that he would know how to do it when he finally flew.

Time passed very quickly, and each day, Dodo became happier. He believed he could fly very soon if he continued to practice with Christine every day.

One morning while he was exercising his wing muscles, he noticed that two eagles had flown to the top of a tree on the mountain peak across from his and begun to build a nest. They were strangers to him. But he didn't worry. Maybe Christine knew them.

Suddenly, Christine appeared, seemingly from out of nowhere. "What are you thinking?" she asked, startling him.

"Christine!" Dodo said. "I was just thinking of you." Dodo spread his right wing and pointed toward the new nest. "Those two eagles settled across the way this morning. Do you know them?"

Christine smiled. "I sure do. That's Mobe and his wife. Mobe is stern, strong. You could learn well if he would agree to teach you to fly. Mobe once worked at a school to teach little eagles how to fly. Perhaps they plan to settle down here for a while. Maybe they'll have children soon." She touched Dodo's wing. "But now it's time to practice."

Dodo followed Christine's instructions, and continued to practice moving his wings and learning the basic skills of flying.

\* \* \*

Just as Christine had predicted, several days later, two little eagles hatched in Mobe's nest. They were blind and weak, crying to the sky. Mobe and his wife spent all day flying back and forth to the nest to feed their children.

Within two days, the little eagles could flap their wings, like they were ready to fly. Mobe and his wife stayed close by to look after their baby eagles. Since Dodo had the eyes and ears of an eagle, he could see and hear Mobe and his family clearly.

"My babies," Mobe was saying in a happy voice. "Would you like to learn to fly now?"

"Yeah, yeah." The babies replied, flapping their weak wings.

"That's good. I will teach each of you separately. After the first of you learns to fly, the other one will wait for a few weeks to start his lessons."

"I want to go first," cried the baby Mobe called Lily.

"No, me!" cried the baby known as Rose.

Mobe shook his head. "No, we will have a contest to decide," he said. "The baby who wins will be the first to fly."

"Yay!" Lily and Rose jumped happily inside their nest.

Mobe smiled. "The game is called 'How to Fly Cross the Mountains in Ten Days.' Do you see these mountains? Do you know how beautiful it is beyond the mountains? You will discover such incredible beauty when you learn to fly. You will be so pleased with what you see. The baby who follows my instruction faithfully will learn to fly and cross the mountains within ten days. Have a good rest and we will see whether Lily or Rose is the lucky bird."

Then Mobe and his children began to eat their lunch.

Dodo, who had heard every word Mobe said, realized the he could also learn to fly by listening to what Mobe told the babies. If he moved closer to Mobe's nest, and studied with the lucky baby, in ten days he would fly across the Rocky Mountains and see the beautiful world from the sky. Dodo couldn't wait to tell Christine the good news.

# Chapter 8

Dodo woke up very early the next morning. It was still dark. He rose from his warm nest to the chill of the predawn air. A few stars still twinkled down on him, but Dodo knew he had to start his dream journey now.

He cleaned his nest and ate a breakfast of corn. Then he walked down the path from his mountain peak so he could climb to the top of Mobe's mountain. If only he could fly, he would be there in no time. Instead, it took him almost a half hour to walk down his mountain and up Mobe's. But he had to get there as early as he could. Mobe had said yesterday that he would choose one of his babies to give flying lessons to this morning. Dodo didn't want to miss the class.

It was the first time Dodo had walked in the dark before sunrise. The world was calm and slightly cold. Dodo made sure he watched for shrubs that might scratch and hurt him in the dull light, or for weak spots in the mountain that might cause a landslide that would carry him down the mountain to the valley below

But Dodo wasn't frightened. He took deep breaths and carefully pushed on. And his mind never stopped to rest. All of his energy was focused on today's flying lessons. He trusted that Mobe would include him in the flying class. After all, Dodo would be an excellent student. He had wings the size of an adult eagle's and sharp eyesight, whereas Lily and Rose were too weak to fly and their eyes were barely open.

Dodo was so excited. In ten days, taught by this superb eagle, he would fly across mountains and seas. It was like magic. He had always dreamed of traveling to the other side of the mountains to see the magic land outside. And now it was about to happen. He could feel that day coming. While thinking these wonderful thoughts, he moved quickly down the mountain, oblivious to the cold and dead quiet.

When he reached the foot of the mountain; the orange sun showed his tender face above the peaks. Dodo stopped to rest. He wiped the sweat that had popped out on his forehead from the exertion, despite the cold, and flapped his wings to the sky.

Such a beautiful day! Sunlight sparkled on the mountains, and a slight breeze picked up, spreading the sunlight's warmth through the chill air. Birds began to sing in the valley. Plants and grasses awoke to smile at Uncle Sun. Dodo was completely happy. "Thank you for giving me a perfect day to achieve my dream!" he said to the sky.

He drank some water from the Green River and washed his face. The reflection of a strong bald eagle looked back, with its sharp beak, straight eyes, and white-crested head. He was a real bald eagle and he would master his flying skills in just ten days. Dodo smiled and promised himself to stop at the river again after he learned to fly.

With his spirit and body refreshed, Dodo continued his magic journey to Mobe's nest high up in a tree on the other mountain peak. It wasn't difficult for Dodo to climb the tree. He had practiced climbing in school, something chickens were taught so they could escape danger on the ground. The sun warmed his body as he climbed.

He wondered what he should do to celebrate at the end of day. Everything pointed to him being one of the first students Mobe would pick to learn to fly. It was such a wonderful day! The warm sun, singing birds, and his own smiling face reflected in the river were only the start. The best was yet to come!

The first thing he would do when he got back to his nest, he decided, was tell Christine the great news. She'd be waiting for him, he knew. She had been so caring and kind to help him since he met her. He couldn't wait to share his happiness with his beautiful friend.

Yes, it would be wonderful. He would fly back to his nest after his lesson and surprise Christine with a big dinner. He would pick some delicious berries from all over, once he could fly, and make gift of them to Christine.

With these happy thoughts in mind, Dodo arrived at Mobe's nest. He was glad to see that Mobe was still sleeping. That meant the lessons hadn't started yet. Dodo found a huge branch to hide behind, where he could easily observe Mobe's movement. He leaned the full weight of his body against it and waited.

Lily and Rose woke up first. They immediately began screaming at their dad to wake up. They nipped at his strong, seven-foot-long wings. Mobe turned in his sleep and almost crushed his lovely baby Lily.

"Daddy, wake up. Wake up. You promised us you would teach us to fly today." Lily and Rose shouted in his ear.

Mobe spread his sleepy wings to the sky, and Lily immediately ran under the huge canopy they created, Rose right behind her.

"So are you ready now, my babies?" Mobe smiled at his lovely children.

"Yes. Yes." Lily and Rose couldn't wait to start their flying program and explore the magic of the sky.

Dodo, behind the branch of the tree, sat up, his heart beating with excitement. He didn't want to miss one word of this flying master's lesson.

"All right, then," said Mobe. "Let's start the first round of our selection process. The eagle who gets the highest mark in today's lesson will be taught in the following ten days how to fly across the mountains. Of course, the other one will have to wait for next term to master her flying skills.

"Before we start our selection, I'll give you a brief introduction about eagle flying. Please listen carefully. Everything I ask you later on will be answered here now. Clear?"

"Clear." Rose and Lily walked closer to their father.

"You will need flying lessons twice in your life," Mobe told them. "The first time is right after you are born, when you're still babies, as you two are. The other time is when you are about forty. Both times will be difficult for you."

Lily and Rose looked puzzled. "But why must we learn to fly again at the age of forty?" Lily asked.

Mobe touched her head with his wing. "Because we eagles must start a new life then. Our beaks, claws, and wings are very old by that time, so we are no longer able to soar through the sky. At that time, you have two choices. You can wait to die, or change into a new bird. If you opt to change, you will fly deep into the mountains and build your nest there. They you must destroy your beak on a hard rock so that a new beak can be born.

"In the same way, you must pull all the claws from your feet so that new ones can grow. And, finally, you must shed all your feathers. Several weeks later, a set of whole new feathers will appear on your wings. This is when you can once again leave the nest and fly again into the blue sky. All this will take one hundred and fifty days.

"During this time, an eagle has only two things to do—gaze at the blue sky from his nest and endure the pain of renewing himself."

"Wow!" cried Rose. "That must be a hard time for an eagle. Unable to fly, or enjoy the beauty of the sky. And having to deal with all that pain at the same time!" Rose couldn't imagine ever turning forty.

"Quite right. It is more difficult than learning to fly for the first time, to be alone like that, totally changing. However, you will learn to deal with that situation when you grow up. I know you'll both be able to handle it when the time comes."

Dodo was very relieved that he was still young and wouldn't have to deal with any of those things for a long time. He was even happier that he wasn't a baby like Rose and Lily. It would be much easier to fly with strong wings like his than their tiny wings.

As he sat there gloating, a small branch growing from the larger branch he was leaning against cracked, and Mobe was immediately on the alert.

37

He jumped in front of his two children, protecting them with his wings. Then, with the babies tucked safely away, he moved closer to the place the sound had come from.

Dodo's heart raced and the blood rushed to his head as Mobe drew nearer and nearer. His face felt like it was on fire. This was the moment that his future began.

Mobe opened his wings and let his children come out of their hiding place when he discovered another eagle standing on the branch of the nearby tree, then he broke the branch between him and Dodo. "Who are you?" he asked the young eagle. Why are you sneaking about, listening to my flying lessons?"

Dodo took a deep breath to calm his nerves. "My name is Dodo," he replied. "And like you, I am an eagle. But I was raised by chickens from birth and never learned to fly."

"It is obvious you are an eagle," Mobe observed. "You look to be about ten years old. Where do you live now? Still with the chickens?"

Dodo admired Mobe's powers of deduction. He had guessed Dodo's age on the very first try.

"No," Dodo replied, answering Mobe's question about his living situation. "I left the chickens and live in a nest on the other side of the Rocky Mountains. I want to learn to fly," he added proudly.

"Well, that is very brave of you," Mobe said. "But I must say, you're awfully old to be learning how to fly." He examined Dodo's wings for a moment. "Although you have two large wings, I can see that they're much too weak to support you in flight. Although you have two yellow claws, they're not very sharp because you've worn them down, walking all the time."

Dodo raised his head: "I know I have many shortcomings," he replied, "but I know I can learn to fly if I try."

Mobe shook his head. "My child, be realistic! You can't achieve your dream with ambition alone. You're better off returning to your adoptive mother and living as a chicken. Unless, of course, you want to do as the old eagles do and change your whole body. But I think that would be a difficult decision, even for an adult eagle. No, son. I'm afraid it's impossible."

With that, Mobe took his daughters and flew off.

Dodo felt terribly confused. How could he walk back to his nest when he had thought he would fly there? He kept playing Mobe's words over and over in his head, looking for a way around them.

How could Mobe believe he should live with the chickens for the rest of his life instead of teaching him how to fly after all Dodo had told him?

It was almost noon, and Uncle Sun was smiling upon the mountains. Red roses and green grass rose happily in Uncle's warmth. But Dodo could hardly see them, he was so upset. Dodo didn't know what to do now.

He wished he never came out here at all. If he hadn't gotten his hopes up about learning to fly, he wouldn't be feeling so terrible right now. It had never occurred to him that Mobe might refuse to teach him.

Only a minute had passed. The sun and beautiful mountains were the same as before. But Dodo's mood was as cold as an iceberg in winter. He should have been celebrating his good fortune today. Instead, he was going home a miserable failure.

# Chapter 9

Christine flew to Dodo's nest early and waited for him to come back with his good news. She cleaned the nest and made a delicious dinner to celebrate Dodo's selection as one of Mobe's flying students.

When Dodo returned, moping and despondent, Christine didn't know what to make of it. "What's the matter with you?" she asked. "Why do you look so sad?"

Dodo didn't know how to tell Christine that Mobe had rejected him as a student. He tried to be brave and not to cry. But Christine's question just reminded him how badly he had failed at realizing his dream.

"I'm sorry," he said. "After all you've done for me, I don't deserve to have you as a friend. I failed, Christine. Mobe won't teach me how to fly." This time he couldn't stop the tears that trickled down his cheeks.

"Oh, Dodo!" Christine said, rushing to put a comforting wing around him. "It will be OK. You'll see. It's not the end of the world. You can try again later."

Dodo shook his head. "No, I don't have a chance," he sobbed. "Not a chance. Mobe said my wings weren't strong enough to support me in flight. He said I should just go back to my adoptive mother unless I thought I could stand the great pain of losing my claws and beak and feathers, like the older eagles."

Christine listened sympathetically, but said nothing. And eventually, Dodo, tired from the day, fell asleep.

Fearing for his safety because of his depressed mood, Christine decided to stay with him in case he needed her when he woke up.

\* \* \*

It was almost noon the next day when Dodo finally woke from his sleep. He seemed to have forgotten the horrible news he received yesterday, as he rubbed his eyes. Then he noticed Christine sitting nearby in the nest. "When did you get here?" he asked.

"It's nice to see you awake," Christine replied. "And to answer your question, I never left. You were so tired and in such a sad mood, I thought I should stay. You look much better now, by the way." Christine smiled, glad to see that Dodo seemed to have gotten over the bad news of yesterday.

Dodo didn't say anything, and soon Christine realized that he hadn't forgotten at all. He looked around the nest for his corn bags and began to make something to eat. Christine joined in, helping him to prepare lunch, trying to brighten his mood. But Dodo was very quiet and withdrawn.

When they finished preparing their food, they took the extra corn and buried it for later. As they dug the holes, Christine couldn't help thinking that it was very strange Dodo was using so much corn for a single lunch.

They ate in silence. Christine tried to make small talk, but she finally stopped when she saw that it was having no effect on Dodo.

After lunch, Dodo left the nest without saying a word to Christine. He stopped to pick some flowers and put them in his feathers. There were so many flowers and plants he had never seen before. For a while, it helped him to forget.

Christine followed behind him, hoping that the beautiful flowers and warm sun would help him forget the pain of yesterday's failure. In a few days, he'd be better, she was sure. She felt better as she watched Dodo smile, jumping at the locusts that scurried around his claws.

But when they returned home for dinner, Dodo withdrew again. He ate his corn in silence, and when dinner was finished he said, "You should go back home now, Christine. Your parents must be worried."

Christine shook her head. "It doesn't matter. I'm worried about you."

"I'm OK. You don't have to," Dodo replied.

Christine looked at him for a minute. "OK, if you're sure you feel better, maybe I will go home," she said. "I'll come back tomorrow."

Dodo could see that Christine was relieved. She knew her parents must be worried about her. "See you tomorrow!" she called as she flew from the nest.

"See you," Dodo called back, and he watched her until she was nothing more than a small speck on the horizon, then he went to sleep.

* * *

For a week, Christine came to see Dodo everyday. And everyday, Dodo played, then ate dinner, then slept. It seemed not only had he forgotten his failure, but also his dream.

Finally, she couldn't take it any longer. "Dodo," she said. "What's wrong with you? Have you forgotten your dream?"

Dodo looked at her like she was crazy. "What dream?" he said, looking totally confused.

"Your dream to fly! It's all you used to talk about, but now you just hang around, wasting time. You don't have to search for food, so all you do is play. What will you do when you have no corn left for dinner anymore?"

A strange look came over Dodo's face. "It's none of your business what I do," he said angrily. "I can't fly because I'm a chicken, and Mobe said I would never learn to fly. I should have stayed with the chickens. At least there I could have been a leader."

Christine frowned, angry now herself. "I don't want to hear your excuses," she said. "What are you doing here if you don't want to learn to fly? I worried about you for the whole week, but you don't even care. All you can do is feel sorry for yourself."

"You're worried about me? I don't deserve it. I could have stayed with the chickens and lived a happy life. But this damn dream destroyed that forever. I lost the chance to become the leader of the chickens. I left my warm, safe home to come to this dangerous place in search of a dream. I didn't even know that Tada wasn't my real mother until a little while ago. I was happy with her. I could have stayed with my best friend Mead. Then I never would have met you and Mobe. I lost everything that mattered to me to chase my dream, and what did it get me? I was defeated even before I began. Not even a master like Mobe thought he could teach me to fly. This is what I get for my efforts. Do you understand what I'm saying? No, because you never felt like this. You were raised by eagles. You can fly." Dodo began to cry.

Christine stared at Dodo for a minute. "You're right. I don't know what you're feeling. I never lived with anyone but the eagles, and I could fly right after I was born, just like Lily and Rose. But remember this, Dodo. No matter who raised you, no matter what happened in your past or will happen in your future, you are a bald eagle. Nothing can change that. So go back to your chicken family, if that's what you want. But you'll always be an eagle who can't fly." She shook her head. "I don't know, Dodo. Do you think eagles were born the masters of the sky? That they can simply spread their wings and soar on the winds under the sun as soon as they're born? That they can do anything they want?

"Well, you're wrong! Eagles meet difficulties and danger everywhere they go. Do you know why eagles build their nests on cliffs or in treetops? It's to protect their children from being preyed upon by others. Their children face such dangers even before they hatch. Although we lay two eggs at a time, there is little chance that both hatchlings will ever grow up. Even as children, they must fight their own siblings to survive.

"And the lucky eagle who happens to win that fight will have to fight others animals as well, day after day, for the rest of his life. Many will lose their lives before they ever fly. And if they manage to survive long enough to fly, they'll have to constantly be on the watch for predators, even human beings, who will attack them without reason. Thousands of our brothers and sisters are killed in accidents while they're flying. But all those dangers and difficulties don't defeat the brave heart of a bald eagle. Rather, they grow braver and stronger. They learn to fly high and fast to stay alive. They learn to fly over the valley or across the river in a flash. The survivors are heroes, who understand the true meaning of soaring into the heavens.

"You feel sorry for yourself because you were raised by chickens and can never learn to fly. Did you ever think of your dying brother? Yes, he was wrong to attack you in the nest. But he is dead, now. He never knew what it meant to fly. But you are still alive. You can still learn to fly if you don't give up.

"Did Mobe's words come as a shock to you? Fair enough. You have some big obstacles to overcome. But do you ever wonder why eagles fly so close to the sun? There are many, many birds, but they all fly much lower than a bald eagle. Do you know why?"

Dodo just looked at her.

"Because true success isn't something you achieve in a day," she told him. "You must overcome many obstacles and difficulties before you finally succeed. If you could become a success that easily, all the birds would dance with the eagles beneath the sun.

Christine sighed. "Look, Dodo. I know things have been tough for you. But I also knew there was something special about you the very first time I met you. I thought you were so brave to follow your dream, and I wanted to help you if I could. I knew how hard it must be to give up the only life you knew to search for your dream. Although there's no way I could understand exactly what you felt, I knew that you were very brave to search for a totally different life in the air when all you had ever known was life on land.

"And I thought how God must love you, the way he brought you Mobe and me so quickly. I thought you would learn to fly in no time. What Mobe told you might be true, but nothing is impossible if you really want it. Miracles do happen.

"But the way you've been acting over this first stumbling block has really upset me. It makes me think I had you all wrong. You'll never learn to fly if you continue to feel sorry for yourself and mope around. For the past week, you've acted like a total loser.

Dodo shrugged. "I'm sorry you feel that way," he said.

Christine shook her head. "That's all you have to say to me? Well, if you want to give up your dream, go ahead. Go back to your chicken family and don't waste any more of my time."

With that, Christine spread her wings and soared into the sky.

# Chapter 10

Christine didn't come to see Dodo the next day, and all Dodo could do was think about what she'd said to him. He stayed by himself all day, feeling lonely and depressed. At night, he stared at the sparkling stars and moon and brushed the tears from eyes.

The night was so long. But it was a good time to think about his past, present and future. Dodo felt that he was standing at the corner of a crossroad. There were two ways that lay in front of him. Dodo thought, if Tada was at his side, he would choose the right way.

Dodo thought about his mother all the time lately. She always stood by him, no matter what happened, whether times were happy or hard. As the night dragged on, Dodo decided that he would go back to see his mom and ask for her advice when the sun rose. The idea excited him.

The only problem was, what to tell her when he went back home. That he didn't want to fly anymore because of Mobe's comments?

No way! He didn't want to tell her that. Mom had told him again and again that he could fly someday if he only dared to try. And to always trust the power of the sky. Whenever he felt alone and powerless, she had told him, dare to ask the sky for help.

Recalling Tada's talk, Dodo raised his eyes to the heavens. He observed the north star sparkling very strong and bright. Bowing his head, he silently prayed to that star. "God, please tell me what I should do next. If you think I should keep trying to make my dream true, please tell me by letting the north star twinkle even brighter.."

Dodo opened his eyes, took a deep breath, and waited for a few seconds. He knew that the master would have to spend a few moments considering his request. He believed that the north star would determine his future and imagined the possible results he might have to face. Knowing that he might lose his dream forever, but ready to face it if that was the star's answer, Dodo looked up.

He couldn't believe his eyes. The star sparkled ten times brighter at him through the calm, dark night. Tears rose to Dodo's eyes. It was his answer. There was someway he could learn to fly. God had sent the answer to him through the north star. But how?

He mulled the problem over for the rest of night. Then, just before dawn, something Mobe said to him gave him the answer. Mobe had said that Dodo's wings and claws had lost their original functions because they had never been used properly. His only chance was to change from the inside out, like the old eagles did. Although it would be very difficult and risky for him, Dodo decided he would take that chance. It was his only hope.

After his momentous decision, Dodo forgot his tiredness and the cold night that surrounded him. There was a fire burning deep in his heart. As soon as the sun rose over the Rocky Mountains, he would begin his plan.

At last, the stars and moon said goodbye to Dodo and went home to sleep after greeting Uncle Sun. It was a beautiful day. Birds sang in the valley, welcoming the new day. The green grass and wild roses turned their smiling faces to the lovely sun.

Dodo collected all the corn sacks from the holes he had hidden them in, and placed them in his nest. Once he shed his feathers and claws he wouldn't be able to leave his home, so he needed to be sure he had enough food.

When everything was ready, Dodo shook his wings. Then he began to pull every last feather from his long wings.

He held his breath and closed his beak tightly to keep from shouting with pain. Tears shimmered in his eyes as blood began to flow from his wings, but he kept on pulling out the feathers. Sweat ran down his face and neck. But every time he experienced the pain of pulling out one of his feathers, he said to himself, "Success is near, success is near," and it helped him to stand the pain.

Still, it was becoming more and more painful for Dodo to pull the feathers from his wings. Each time he yanked out a feather, it took all the energy in his body and spirit to withstand the excruciating pain. Bleeding profusely, his body drenched in sweat, Dodo began to weaken and then to swoon.

When he regained consciousness, he couldn't remember where he was for a moment. Then he noticed the pile of feathers on the ground beside his nest. His body was just bare skin, now. He was a bald bird in the wind. Maybe that's why people called his kind bald eagles, he thought.

Dodo almost laughed hysterically when that flashed through his mind. But he wasn't finished yet. There were still his claws to deal with.

Taking a deep breath, he found a hard rock beside the nest and dragged his claws across it roughly. The pain made him want to cry out, but he stifled the scream in his throat. Pieces of yellow claw fell from his body and spread into the winds.

Once his claws were all gone, Dodo took a final breath and fell into an exhausted sleep.

He slept for many days, waking only to take some corn and drink some water from the dew on the grass and flowers near his nest. Then he fell asleep again to recover his energy for the total change.

\* \* \*

For two months, Dodo lived like this. Then one day he woke up to find down growing on his wings and face and body. New yellow claws were growing from his feet, including two sharp claws he had never had before.

Dodo was very excited about the change in his body, and began to dream of flying again. He wanted to ask Christine to give him another flying lesson soon. But he hadn't seen Christine since she flew away that final time, leaving him alone during his transformation.

Maybe she was really upset by the way Dodo had acted and would never return. Whenever he thought about her, he imagined how he would apologize to her for the way he had acted.

Meanwhile, his food had nearly disappeared. It was already fall, and Dodo knew he couldn't spend the whole winter without corn. He decided he should travel down the mountain and find more.

\* \* \*

The days passed, with Dodo watching Mobes' baby eagles learning to fly from across the mountain while he grew stronger and stronger every day.

One day, Dodo noticed a group of chickens walking toward the banks of the Green River. They marched in a straight line toward the water, following a leader with a flag. Dodo couldn't believe he could see the chicken group from this distance. But then he realized that such sharp vision was normal for a bald eagle.

Dodo grew excited. The way those chickens walked in a straight line, Dodo knew they must be students—his classmates and friends. He was so happy to see them! He wanted to rush in front of the group and say hello. But then he remembered that he shouldn't walk anymore, now that his new sharp claws had grown in. Still, he wanted to see his friends, so he cleaned his nest and climbed down the mountain.

The song the chickens were singing grew louder as he approached them. It was one of his favorite songs from school. He even remembered the lyrics. He couldn't wait to say hi to everyone.

But when he drew near, the chickens started squawking with fright and ran to find shelter. Dodo couldn't understand why his friends were running away from him, but he was hot and tired from his climb down the mountain, so decided to get a drink.

He reached the banks of the Green River and began to dip his beak into the river for a cool drink. It was the first time in a long time that he had cool, clear river water to drink. But as he bent over the water, he caught sight of his reflection and understood why the chickens had feared him.

There, in the river, was the reflection of a true bald eagle, with its sharp beak, wide feathers, and yellow claws. Not a trace of his chicken self was left.

North winds blew across his body and he experienced a chill in his heart. The old Dodo was gone forever. He was an eagle, now, and eagles and chickens were not friends. He had to say goodbye to yesterday and his old friends. He had to forget the past and welcome the future! The door to yesterday was closed.

The north wind grew colder. Dodo searched for food at the foot of the mountains, but couldn't find any. Heavy, dark clouds hid the sun. It would rain soon. Dodo decided he'd better get back to his nest.

The winds were bitter on the road to his nest, and Dodo had to fight them all the way. Without any source of food, he wondered how he would be able to make it through the winter. He obviously couldn't depend on his chicken friends anymore.

Dodo worried about this all way home. Then, when he reached his nest, he discovered some blood there. Plus, where the nest had been empty when he left, it was now filled with packages. Wondering what it all meant, Dodo opened one of the bags carefully, and his mouth dropped open.

The packages were full of corn and grain, his favorite winter foods. He wouldn't have to worry about food for the winter after all. These sacks would easily feed him for six more months. But who brought them, and why was their blood in his nest? Only Christine knew he lived there. So it must have been Christine who brought him the food. But why did she leave before he got back? Was she still angry with him? Then why bring him food at all? And if it wasn't Christine, who *had* brought it?

Dodo pondered this for several minutes, without success. He supposed it didn't matter who had brought the food. It gave him that much more time to learn to fly.

By nightfall, Dodo had forgotten the sad experience of the morning, and was enjoying his dinner beneath the moon, when he heard a far-off voice call his name. He stopped mid-bite, left his nest, and looked around.

The voice sounded so familiar. Dodo turned his head, listening to the echo that moved throughout the dark mountains. Then, suddenly, he felt someone take hold of him from behind, and say his name.

"Dodo, is that you?" the voice asked, and Dodo finally recognized the voice—it was Mead!

Dodo turned around, returning Mead's hug. "Yes, it's me," he replied. "I can't believe you found me, and had the courage to approach me in the dark when you weren't sure who it was. How are you? What are you doing here?"

Mead sighed. "It's a long story, Dodo. The reason I'm here... The reason I dared to approach a bald eagle when I wasn't exactly sure it was you....Well, I'm afraid I have some bad news. Your mother, Tada, was attacked by a wolf this morning. She's in a coma."

Dodo felt first pain and then rage. "What do you mean, she's in a coma? Didn't I ask you to look after my mom before I left? What have you been doing?" Dodo held Mead tightly with his sharp claws.

"I'm sorry, I'm sorry," Mead said, his voice shaking with fear. "Please don't hurt me, Dodo. Tada was attacked by a wolf on the way to see you. She insisted on bringing you corn for the winter, and she wouldn't wait for me to come with her.."

Dodo loosened his claws. There was blood on Mead's body where the claws had clutched. Tada had been attacked bringing him food. If only she had seen him at the Green River, the attack could have been prevented.

"Forgive me, Mead," Dodo said, feeling ashamed. "I'm just so upset about my mother. How is she? Did the doctor say she'll recover?"

Mead shook his head. "She is still in danger. I wanted to come see you sooner, before all this happened, but Tada said it would interrupt your flying lessons and stopped me. But even in her coma, she calls your name from time to time. I knew I had to find you and bring you back."

"Thank you, Mead. You did the right thing," Dodo said. "Let's go." In his haste to get to his mother, he completely forgot that he was still recovering himself.

With that, the two set out down the mountain. Tada's face and voice echoed in Dodo's mind as he and Mead hurried back home, and in his heart Dodo kept saying, "Hold on, Mom, I'm coming. I'm coming, Mom."

# Chapter 11

It was almost midnight when Mead and Dodo reached Tada's house. Jude was standing near Tada's bed when Dodo entered the room. Dodo rushed forward and fell on his knees in front of his mother, tears falling as he touched her hand.

Tada lay on her bed, her body trembling with fever. There were some small wounds on her pale face, perhaps made as she ran through the grasses, trying to escape the wolf. Her mouth opened and closed, opened and closed, saying something Dodo couldn't understand.

Dodo gently shook her: "Mom, mom, it's me," he said. "Wake up, please wake up." But Tada remained in her coma, repeating her murmured words.

Dodo turned to Jude. "Aunt, what did the doctor say?" he asked.

Jude shook her head sadly. "Your mother's leg was mangled by a wolf when she started off to the mountains to bring you food for the winter. She managed to escape him, and if she had just taken herself home right away, she would have been all right. But she insisted on delivering the food to you. It took a lot out of her. She lost a lot of blood. The doctor said tonight will be very dangerous for her, and that we must pray for a miracle."

"No, I won't believe it. Mom will be OK! She has to be."

Jude touched his wing. "Child, please let her rest. Don't disturb her any more tonight. It's best that you go to your room and try to sleep. I'll take care of your mom and call you if anything happens."

Dodo shook his head. "Thank you, Jude. You've been very kind. But I'll stay with my mother tonight. You go back to your house with Mead, now, and get some rest."

Jude looked from Dodo to Tada and back again. "Well, all right, then. But make sure you call me if you need help. We'll leave the light on. I know your mother will be OK once she sees you."

Jude and Mead left Tada's room, closing the door behind them. They returned home and lit a yellow candle so that Dodo would see a light in the dark night, while Dodo sat alone in the dark with his mother.

Once Mead and Jude were gone, Dodo placed a wing on Tada's shoulder and bowed his head. "Please be OK, Mom," he prayed. "Please wake up. It's Dodo. If you'll only wake up, I'll stay here with you for the rest of my life." Dodo's prayer and Tada's breathing were the only sounds.

The night seemed very long, as if time stood still. Dodo's life flashed before his eyes, memories of happy times with his mother

49

It was his mother who hugged him and encouraged him to go forward when he lost the locust-catching game.

It was his mother who made him pots of delicious soups after he had studied hard all day in school.

It was his mother who told him about who he really was before he became part of the chicken family, who changed his depression over being different from the other chickens into a dream that he could one day fly.

It was his mother who taught him to be a brave chick no matter what difficulties he faced in life and to live the life he loved.

It was his mother who turned his darkness into light, and who fought a cruel wolf so that he would have food for the winter.

The more Dodo thought about the things Tada had done for him, the more his heart ached. He couldn't stop the tears that came to his eyes and dropped onto Tada's face.

But even as he searched for a handkerchief to wipe the salty drops from his mother's cheek, she stirred from a dream and opened her eyes. "Is that you, my Dodo?" she asked weakly.

"Mom!" Dodo cried, hardly able to believe his eyes. "Yes, Mom, it's me. Dodo. I'm back." He quickly wiped the tears from his eyes, so she wouldn't see.

"Am I dreaming?" Tada touched the face of this bald eagle with her weak wings.

"No, I'm really here. It's Dodo."

His mother managed a smile. "I just dreamed about you yesterday. I went to your nest in the Rocky Mountains. I didn't find you or the purple ribbon there, so I thought perhaps you flew somewhere to search for food. I was very happy to think you had already mastered the ability to fly. On the way home, I ran across a wolf. He chased me. I had to run faster and faster. I was very scared in my dream"

Dodo couldn't hold back his tears. All his regrets and gratitude poured out of him. "It's my fault, Mom. If I never dreamed of becoming a bald eagle, you wouldn't have been attacked by a wolf. Please forgive me, and I will stay with you from now on, and never think about flying again."

Tada touched his cheek. "My child, it was just a dream. Never talk about giving up your flying unless you really don't want to do it anymore."

Their talking woke up Jude and Mead next door, and soon they came by with soup for Tada. Jude opened the windows beside the bed. The sun was just beginning to rise, and a weak light poured into the room along with a some sweet, fresh air, making everyone feel better.

"Oh, Tada!" cried Jude. "I'm so happy to see you awake. We were so afraid for you. You were unconscious for the whole night—a coma the doctor said—and you just kept calling Dodo's name. Rest here, and I'll heat some soup for your breakfast." Jude donned an apron and went to the kitchen with Mead to get breakfast ready for everyone.

When Jude and Mead went into the kitchen, Tada said, "Dodo, stay and have breakfast with us. But after that, you must return to the mountain."

Dodo didn't say anything. Tada said that now, but maybe she would feel different after breakfast. He went into the kitchen and helped prepare the table.

During breakfast, the four talked about the changes that had taken place after Dodo left. Mead had graduated from chicken school and become an adult guard in the chicken family. Jude and Tada took long walks together during the day when there was no work for them to do. Then Tada and Jude asked about Dodo's life in the mountains. Dodo told them he had made all kinds of plans to start flying in the springtime.

After breakfast, Jude and Mead prepared dessert in the kitchen. Dodo arranged the table and talked with his mom. "Mom, I want to stay with you for a while," he said.

"But why Dodo?" Tada asked, surprised. "Don't you want to return to the mountains and find your dream?"

"I don't want you worry about me any more," Dodo told her. "I've missed a lot of happy times with you since I left for the mountains, and I want to stay with you from now on. I've decided to give up my dream."

Tada sighed. "I suppose that's all right, if flying is no longer what you want to do," Tada replied in a weak voice. "But never let your dream be disrupted by an external situation. It is difficult to achieve our dreams, because we must face many difficulties and frustrations before we finally succeed. On the other hand, it's not as hard as we suppose when we are determined to overcome every obstacle that lies in our path."

"But, Tada, is it worth the price of possibly never seeing you again?" Dodo asked, worried about Tada's health.

"That's for you to decide," Tada told him. "But no matter what you decide, always live the life you want to live. Strive for your dream and don't worry about me. Soon, you will be able to fly to see me. The next time I see you, I hope you will be flying with your purple ribbon tucked in your claws."

Realizing that Tada was right, and he must follow his dream, Dodo said goodbye, knowing he was leaving her in good hands with Jude and Mead to look after her. He looked back one last time with tears and his eyes, then returned to his nest, vowing that he would fly back soon to see his mother.

\* \* \*

Weeks passed, and Dodo, determined to succeed, turned into a new eagle. He concentrated on observing other birds in flight over the cliffs every day. And he carefully watched and listened to Mobe from a distance when Mobe taught flying to his children.

Dodo didn't remember the exact day that Christine returned to his nest. She came back one day when Dodo was exercising his wings.

"Dodo!" she cried. "Is it really you? You've completely changed. Wow! New feathers, new claws... soon you'll be flying like the rest of the eagles."

Dodo smiled. "Yeah. I followed Mobe's advice and changed my whole body. I figured I should start a new life and learn to fly. So how are you? I haven't seen you for such a long time." Dodo lowered his head. "Are you still angry with me?"

Christine brushed his face with her wing. "No, I'm not angry, Dodo. I had to take care my little brother after he was born, so I couldn't fly far from the nest for months. But now my mother has taken over my duties, so I have more free time."

Dodo looked up. "I'm so glad to hear that. So, can I ask you something? Would you mind teaching me some basic flying skills?"

Christine smiled. "I'd love to. I helped to teach my little brother."

\* \* \*

For the next few weeks, Christine taught Dodo how to fly. The first thing he had to do, she told him, was make his wings strong. So every day, Dodo would flap his wings one hundred times, getting them ready to fly.

By the end of the week, Dodo was easily flapping his wings a hundred times or more. Christine thought it was time for him to try to use his wings to fly. So she led him to the cliff near his nest.

When they reached the cliff, Dodo looked down at the valley below. It was so deep, he couldn't see the bottom. Cold winds blew in his face. He was frightened, and unconsciously stepped back from the cliff.

Christine pushed him forward again. "It's time for you to fly," she said. "Go for it."

"I'm not sure I'm ready," Dodo replied, taking a tentative step forward.

Christine decided she couldn't wait any longer. She opened her wings wide and slammed them into Dodo's body. Dodo teetered on the edge of the cliff for a moment, then fell off.

"Help! Help!" he cried as he plummeted toward the earth. But Christine just watched him fall.

Realizing he was on his own, Dodo began to flap his wings. But no matter how hard he flapped, nothing seemed to happen. He tried turning this way and that, flapping his wings faster and then slower. But still he fell.

At the last minute, Christine dove off the cliff like a bolt of lightning and grabbed hold of Dodo's wings with her claws, carrying him back to the cliff again.

Dodo was shaking with fright and soaked in sweat by the time his claws touched solid ground again. Christine helped him back to the nest, where he lay down, taking deep breaths until he felt better.

"Are you OK?" Christine asked him. "That was your first flying experience. All eagles are afraid when they first start flying. But once you overcome your fear, you'll enjoy the pleasure of flying and being in harmony with the air."

"I know. I'm OK," Dodo assured her. "I'll fly better next time."

But whatever happened, Dodo knew he would never forget his first attempt at flying.

# Chapter 12

The more he practiced his lessons, the more Dodo began to feel comfortable with the idea of flying. Christine suggested that he find a soft place to land, so he wouldn't be hurt even if he fell to the ground. Even so, Dodo still had cuts all over his body from his many failures. But he understood that the more he practiced, the closer he would become to the air and sky.

Dodo felt better about himself now. He didn't feel so alone when Christine wasn't at his side. Rose and Lily often come to see him practice. They'd laugh at him when he fell. The fact was, Dodo's flying was pretty bad sometimes. But he didn't let their jibes bother him. Rather, he would ask them for advice so he could learn from his mistakes.

One time, he was practicing the flying moves Christine had taught him. He was very tired that day, and was doing quite poorly trying to fly against the wind. There were two net barriers set 100 yards apart that he was trying to get over. But no matter how hard he tried, he failed every time. He decided he was going to try one last time he before giving up for the day.

He took a deep breath and spread his wings, then drew his claws to his belly and rose into the air, as Christine had taught him. He flapped his wings faster and faster. Soon the first barrier was right in front of him—he was almost there. The air current was lifting his feathers, and he knew it was the right time to fly over the barrier. He gathered all his energy and began his ascent. He was so excited! Then one of his claws hooked the net and he began to fall.

He landed hard on the ground, face first. His face was streaked red with mud. Lily and Rose began to laugh hysterically. As they returned to their nest, they couldn't stop talking about how funny Dodo looked.

Then, suddenly, Lily ran back to Dodo, waving her wings frantically. "Dodo! Dodo!" she cried. "Please help Rose. She was laughing and missed her footing when we were walking up the cliff road. She's falling.!"

"What?" Dodo jumped up and ran to the edge of the cliff. Rose was falling toward the valley floor.

Dodo looked angrily at Lily. "Can't you fly?" he demanded. "I thought your father taught you how to fly.

Lily shook her head. "No, neither of us can fly yet."

"Where's Christine?" Dodo asked, looking around anxiously, hoping that Christine had stopped by. But she was nowhere to be seen.

"What am I supposed to do?" Dodo cried to the heavens. "I can't fly down to the valley. I've tried it again and again. Tell me what to do!"

At that moment, his eyes met Rose's as she plummeted to the ground, and he remembered how Tada had saved his life when he'd fallen from his nest those many years ago. He remembered how twice Christine had saved him from crashing to the ground.

He took one last look at Rose, and dove, knowing that if he didn't fly, they would both die. And suddenly, his wings began to flap, and he stopped thinking about anything but saving the baby eagle. Nearer and nearer he flew. Finally, he was so close that he opened his claws and tried to catch Rose's wings, but he missed. Rose kept falling.

Dodo turned around and aimed more carefully this time, adjusting his speed to match Rose's fall. This time, he managed to catch Rose's wings and hold her, just before she hit the ground. Then he took a deep breath, flapped his strong wings, and began to carry her back up the cliff to her nest.

But an air current was pushing down on him, making it very difficult to fly. He forced himself to go on. The air pushed and shoved him, slamming him into the rocks. Still, he kept hold of Rose, ignoring the blood that dripped off his wings to the valley, and continued his flight up and up, until at last he reached the edge of the cliff and was able to set Rose down on the ground.

Lily and Rose hugged each other and cried for a long time. And Dodo, exhausted from the exertion, dragged himself to his nest and fell asleep.

\* \* \*

When he awoke the next afternoon, Dodo was very hungry. He tried to get up to get something to eat. But as soon as he moved, a sharp pain shot through his right wing. He blinked against the bright sun that shone in his eyes. Then suddenly a shadow appeared, blocking the sun. It was Christine.

"Are you feeling any better?" She asked, laying some corn and a leaf full of water in the nest beside him.

"I can't move my right wing," Dodo said. "What's the matter with it?"

"You hurt it on the rocks when you saved Rose's life yesterday. I know it hurts, but you'll be OK in a few weeks. Just try not to move around too much. You need a good rest before you fly again. But don't worry. I'll take care of you in the meantime."

Dodo ate some of the corn and drank some water. "So what about Rose and Lily? Did they get back home safely?"

"They're OK. Mobe wants to visit you when you're feeling better."

Dodo turned onto his other side to ease the pain of his wounded wing. Then he fell asleep again.

\* \* \*

The next morning, he was awakened by a conversation between Christine and another eagle. Dodo tried to get up. Christine and the other eagle, who it turned out was Mobe, saw him trying to move, and ran to his side to help him.

"You remember Mobe, don't you, Dodo?" Christine said. "He came here this morning to see you."

"Yes," Dodo said. "It's nice to see you again, Mobe."

Christine stood at the edge of the nest. "I'm going out to get some water," she said. "You two can talk." Then she flew off.

As soon as she was gone, Mobe said, "Dodo, Rose and Lily told me what happened. I'm here to thank you for saving Rose's life. And I'm very sorry that you were hurt in that endeavor." Mobe glanced at Dodo's wounded wings.

"It doesn't matter. I was very happy I was able to save Rose." Dodo raised his body on his good wing and let the sun shine on his face. He felt better now.

"I'm sorry for what I said to you," Mobe said, looking ashamed. "And for my children making fun of you when you were learning to fly. To my thinking, you're a true eagle."

"That's all right, Mobe. The fact is, I wouldn't be able to fly if it wasn't for your instruction."

Mobe smiled. "You are truly a brave eagle. I am proud to be part of your story. You learned to fly despite what I told you. Well done!"

"Thank you," Dodo said.

"No, there's nothing to thank me for," Mobe replied. "But there's something I want to do for you. I want to tell you some secrets about flying. Christine and many of our brother eagles learned to fly through practice and failure. The more they practiced, the quicker they mastered the art of flying. But actually, there are some other methods to help you learn to fly very fast." Mobe smiled.

Dodo's eyes gleamed. "Secrets? What are these secrets? Could you please tell me now?"

Mobe shrugged. "Why not? You have proved yourself worthy." He sat down at the edge of the nest, and leaned in close to Dodo. "To watch a bald eagle soar through the sky is one of the most beautiful sights in nature. The ability you must master is not only how to flap your wings to rise in the air, but also how to glide on the wind, becoming part of it.

"First, you should spread your wings to their full length and never be afraid. Always look up! The higher your eyes go, the higher you will fly."

"Second, always go against the wind. You can't control your direction when you fly in the same direction as the wind. When you fly into the wind, you will learn how to take advantage of it and fly effortlessly. Learning to use the air currents will help you fly to great heights."

Dodo listened carefully, memorizing Mobe's valuable information. He wanted to leave the nest right now and put this knowledge into action, but Mobe shook his head.

"I know what you're thinking, Dodo," he said. "Don't try to use this knowledge until you are completely well. For now, just practice in your mind."

"In my mind?" Dodo said, puzzled.

"Yes. Go over these lessons in your mind. Try to feel the wind and how you move within it. Never look down on this kind of practice. The more you fly in your mind, the more successful your true flights will be later on. Get well, Dodo. I'll come back to see you soon."

With that, Mobe touched Dodo's wing and flew into the sky.

* * *

A week later, Dodo began to leave his nest for short periods of time to exercise his wings. Christine told him that he should be able to fly again within the month. It was good news. But some other things Christine told him weren't so good.

"I won't be here to see you for awhile," she said right before she left.

"Why not?" Dodo asked, hardly believing his ears. Christine was always here when he needed her.

"It's nearing winter," she replied. "My family and I are flying south."

"But you'll be back when spring comes."

Christine shrugged. "Perhaps. We may settle in the south, because there are so many eagles killed by illegal hunters here. We've lost many friends. I'm sorry to tell you this way, but I have to follow my parents this time."

Dodo didn't know what to say. "Well, I wish you a good trip," was all he could come up with.

Christine looked at him for a few minutes, tears glistening in her eyes. "I'll miss you," she said. "You'll be in my thoughts. I just wish I had more time to see you before I go."

"When do you leave?" Dodo asked, fighting back tears himself.

"Soon. There's a snowstorm coming. We have to leave before it gets here, or it will be too hard to fly." Christine hugged Dodo tightly. "Take care of yourself."

"You, too," Dodo replied. Then he turned his face away so he wouldn't have to watch Christine fly out of his life.

* * *

The following days were lonely for Dodo. He couldn't practice his flying because of his wounded wing. So he concentrated on imagining every aspect of flying, as Mobe had told him. Even so, thoughts of Christine kept interrupting his practice.

Without Christine, he wouldn't be alive right now, or have learned how to fly. Her kindness and beautiful smile were always on his mind. He couldn't stop himself from wanting to find her. The trouble was, he didn't know where she was headed, other than that it was south of his nest. So he tried his best to forget her and focus his attention on learning to fly.

Mobe and his family came to say goodbye the day before the big storm was due to hit. Mobe examined Dodo's wing and said happily, "It should be OK in about a week. Don't try to use your wings until then. My family and I are flying south before the storm. You'd better find a safer and more comfortable place to spend the winter yourself."

"I can stand the winter here," Dodo replied sullenly. "But tell me, how do I know where to go if I decide to fly south?"

"Your intuition will tell you," Mobe replied. "Don't assume something is difficult before you try it. Trust your intuition. It's easier than thinking when you give it free rein. Let your intuition guide you, and you'll find your way."

Dodo watched as Mobe and his family flew into the distance. The mountains were very quiet. It seemed that all the animals had gone into hibernation. Dodo struggled with the question of whether to stay where he was, or to find Christine. He let the question sit in his heart, waiting for a sign.

Later that night, Dodo was awakened by a fierce storm. Snow blanketed the Rocky Mountains. Dodo held his wings tightly against himself and tried to fall sleep again. But he couldn't sleep with Christine on his mind.

She was flying south with her parents at that very moment. Maybe the Mobe and his family were with them.

"If my wing is OK, I'm going to try to find Christine." Dodo decided.

The storm grew worse. The snow was a sheet of white before Dodo's eyes. It was an obstacle between him and Christine. Seeing how bad it was, Dodo thought that he'd never see Christine again if he didn't take action now.

With that in mind, he grabbed the purple ribbon Tada had given him, jumped from his warm nest, and spread his wings. He ignored the pain in his right wing and flew into the air. The falling snow fought his ascent. It took all his effort to fly beyond the cliff.

Behind the storm, a warm airflow was pushing on his left wing. Dodo realized the warm air must be coming from the south. He flew along the cliff, rising further and further into the sky, heading south, and the snow soon turned into a cold, beating rain. Dodo knew he had to keep his focus and stay on course, or he would be in big trouble.

But the driving rain beat against his wounded wing and inhibited his flying. Dodo couldn't find his way in the heavy rain and was starting to lose his breath.

He shook the raindrops off his wings and adjusted his flying speed. *Remember what Mobe told you,* he thought. *Follow your intuition.* Then he flew higher and higher, finding his way out of one rain cloud only to find himself in another.

The storm stayed with him the whole night. Then, suddenly, a ray of sunshine broke through the clouds.

Dodo flew against the wind to pick up an air current, and let it carry him, enjoying the thrill of gliding on the air for the first time. He was free!

The air current kept him buoyed so Dodo didn't need to flap his wings anymore to fly. Instead, he adjusted the angle of the wings to the changing winds, and soared through the clouds.

The sun rose from the sea, and gave its first smile to the only bird in the air, a bald eagle gliding on the wind. To the north, snow glistened on the Rocky Mountains and Green River. It was the first Dodo ever enjoyed his beautiful mountains from the distant sky.

The Rocky Mountains was wearing a white dress after the snowstorm. The beating sun had started the snow melting, and several waterfalls rushed down the mountain to wash the snow from the grass and plants. The Green River was clean and clear, washed by the melting snow. The trees by the river immediately shed their white uniform and welcomed the sun. The sky was pure blue, with wisps of white cloud.

Dodo flew in and out of the clouds, playing a game with them. He no longer felt tired, just relaxed and joyful soaring through the sky.

Down below, a long river caught his eye. The farther Dodo flew along the river, the warmer the air became. He knew he was headed in the right direction.

Then, suddenly, he heard a voice calling to him, "Dodo, come here with us."

He turned his head and saw some bald eagles flying to the left of him. It was Mobe, Mobe's wife Nina, and the two girls. Dodo was thrilled to see his mentor and flew closer. "Mobe and Nina, Lily, Rose!" he cried.

Mobe grinned. "It's wonderful to see you! I knew you would be a great bald eagle someday."

Dodo smiled back. "Have you seen Christine?" he asked.

"She's ahead of us, about five miles."

"Great! I'm going to fly ahead to find her."

"Good luck!" Mobe and his family said.

Dodo said goodbye and flew ahead to find Christine. He found an air current to help him, and flew like the wind to catch up with the group.

After a while he spotted them, six eagles flying in a group about two miles ahead of him. He realized that the last one was Christine.

Suddenly, the group changed course and Christine became the leader. Dodo was growing tired by this time, and couldn't keep up with them. Christine was flying farther and farther away.

"Christine, I'm coming!" Dodo shouted, hoping she would pick up his words.

\* \* \*

Christine, leading the group, thought she heard someone calling her name. She couldn't be certain, but it sounded like Dodo.

Christine turned her head and flew in a circle so she could see who was calling her. In the distance she spotted a lone eagle with a purple ribbon in his claws.

It had to be Dodo. "It's Dodo, it's Dodo!" Christine excitedly told her family. "Slow down." The group slowed to a near stop in the air as Christine flew back to meet Dodo. Then she returned with him, the two of them flying shoulder to shoulder.

They stayed by each other's side until they reached the main group. Christine introduced Dodo to her family and friends. When she introduced him to an eagle named Ling, that eagle stared at Dodo's purple ribbon and said, "Where did you get that?"

"I've had it since I was a child," Dodo told him.

Ling pointed the ribbon out to her husband, Jia, and the two of them flew closer to Dodo.

"Oh my God!" Jia cried when they drew closer. "It is you. Our baby. You're still alive! We've searched for you these many years, after coming home from our hunting trip and finding you gone. Dodo, my child. This is your father, Jia, and I am your mom, Ling."

Dodo finally realized why Tada gave him the purple ribbon to carry when he flew. It was a signal to his parents that it was him. He cried for happiness to find his true parents.

The four of them flew together while Dodo told them the story about how he had fallen from the nest and Tada had saved him. "You must meet Tada," he said.

"Yes, we wish to thank her," Ling replied.

"I'll go with you." Christine said, wanting to meet Tada, too.

\* \* \*

Tada and her neighbors were sweeping the snow from the ground around their houses when suddenly they heard screaming from the sky.

Tada looked up, and what she saw brought tears to her eyes. There was a bald eagle carrying a purple ribbon flying down to them.

"Dodo, Dodo." Tada jumped for joy. Her neighbors, seeing the eagles diving toward them, took flight, running to find shelter. They thought Tada must have gone crazy, waiting for those eagles like that.

"Mom, it's me!" Dodo said, landing on the snow-covered ground and hugging Tada.

The other chickens looked on in amazement, dumbfounded that Tada could kiss a bald eagle without being killed.

Dodo pulled Christine closer to him and introduced her. "Mom, this is Christine, my friend," he said.

"What a beautiful girl!" Tada hugged Christine.

"And these are my parents," Dodo said, introducing Jia and Ling.

The two eagles smiled. "Thank you for saving our child," Ling said.

"Yes," Jia agreed. "You will be friends of the eagles forever for what you have done."

Tada thanked them for their graciousness, then gestured with her wings for her neighbors to come over.

Hesitantly, the other chickens moved closer.

"This is Dodo," Tada said, proudly introducing her son. "He has become the eagle he was born to be and flown here to see me."

"Dodo?" one of the chickens said. Soon, all of them surrounded Tada and Dodo, celebrating Dodo's return. They didn't have to worry for their safety anymore, now that Dodo was there to protect them. They lifted Tada to their shoulders and held her up to the sky, cheering because she had raised this wonderful eagle in a chicken family.

But too soon, it was time for Dodo to head south again. "Go where you must," Tada said, touching his cheek. "I'll wait for your next visit." Then she hugged him tight.

Dodo kissed his mom. "I'll be back soon," he promised. Then, with Christine and his parents beside him, he soared into the air. "Sky, please show me the horizon," he said, and with his new family, he flew toward the mountains in the distance.

# Tell, Give & Win- with *When Your Heart Seeks the Sky*

Dear Reader,

Thank you for reading *When Your Heart Seeks the Sky,* the simple story of Dodo and the journey that changed his life. Thousands of people - just like you - have already enjoyed this touching story, and are learning the true meaning of giving and sharing.

*When Your Heart Seeks the Sky* is becoming one of the fastest growing bestsellers, thanks to people like you. Through a grassroots, word-of-mouth effort, people are giving and recommending this book to friends and family members - and as a result, are being rewarded with free travel, free books, free iPODs, and much, much more!

**You Can Win!**

When you recommend this book, you can score big prizes! Here's how: Tell your family and friends to visit http://www.amazon.com or http://www.bn.com and search for *When Your Heart Seeks the Sky.* Then send their names and email addresses to share@heartseeks.com, and when their order comes in, you'll automatically be entered in a drawing to win one of these fabulous prizes:

• *Spiritual Marketing* and *The Greatest Money-Making Secret In History* Joe Vitale's 2 Amazon Bestsellers, a $30 value - Yours FREE!

• "*When You Can Walk On Water, Take The Boat,*" the award-winning book by John Harricharan, retails for $50 - but its yours FREE when you tell friends and family about *When Your Heart Seeks The Sky.*"…As delightful and profound as the title. It's one book you'll want to sit down and read in an evening, marking comments and sentences as you go." — Seattle New Times

• "*Think Your Way To Success" e-course* Mary Anne Thomas, author of *Ask and You Shall Receive* and the *Power of Creative Prayer* is offering you a free enrollment in her four-week e-class, *Think Your Way to Success,* valued at $500. Mary Anne is a well-known speaker on national radio and

TV, and has been widely published in newspapers like the New York Times. Her *Think Your Way to Success* class drew standing room only when it was first offered, and it's not currently available, except to purchasers of *When Your Heart Seeks the Sky.* With this e-class, you'll be able to identify your dreams, go for them, and actually manifest signs of their appearance by the end of the four weeks.

PLUS:

• *5 paperback bestsellers from NY Times Bestseller list* - valued at $100. One lucky reader a month will receive 5 different fiction books from the New York Times Bestseller list.

• *The incomparable iPOD,* with a suggested manufacturer's price of $399, will be given to one lucky reader a month.

• *A one-of-a-kind trip to Yunnan, China,* worth $8000 - yes, $8000! One lucky reader will win a one-week, all-expenses paid trip to Yunnan, China in October of 2005.

The more people who buy - or the more copies <u>you</u> buy - the greater your chances to win!

Don't Wait - another FREE Bonus is waiting for you right now!

<u>Refer 10 friends TODAY and we'll automatically send you a free surprise gift!</u> Or order 10 books for yourself, and receive the same surprise gift - valued at $300!

I'm offering these great gifts because I believe the best kind of advertising is word-of-mouth. I could spend thousands of dollars on advertising and marketing campaigns, but instead I want to reward you, the reader, for spreading the word about my book.

I want to hear your comments about how my thoughtful story *When Your Heart Seeks the Sky* moved you. Please visit my site and share your thoughts at http://www.heartseeks.com or email me directly at author@heartseeks.com. I'm looking forward to hearing from you.

Help me prove that the best sales in the world come from people just like you! Tell, Give & Win - tell your friend to visit Amazon.com or BN.com and order *When Your Heart Seeks the Sky* now!

Sincerely,

Wang Jian

P.S. For orders of 100 or more, from any bookstore, company or individual, you will receive a special discount PLUS a surprise thank-you gift! Just contact author@heartseeks.com and we'll process your order – and send your gift – right away!

P.P.S. Remember - winning big prizes is as easy as 1-2-3!

1. Tell your friends to visit http://www.amazon.com or http://www.bn.com and search for *When Your Heart Seeks the Sky*. Or you can visit and place orders for additional copies to give to family and friends.

2. Send their names and email addresses to share@heartseeks.com, and when their order comes in, you'll automatically be entered to win one of several amazing prizes, including a $399 iPOD and $8000 all-expense paid trip to China!

3. Refer 10 friends to http://www.amazon.com or http://www.bn.com or order 10 copies for yourself - and receive a FREE surprise gift.

Act TODAY - WIN today… it's just that easy!

We would love to hear from you.
Read great testimonials on When Your Heart
Seeks the Sky or submit your own story.
Visit www.heartseeks.com

# About the Book

In this charming fable, a young chicken, Dodo, wonders why his friends always make fun of him. They laugh at his sharp beak and long feathers. The tease him mercilessly.

Then one day, Dodo sees an eagle soaring in the skies above him. If only I could be like that eagle, he thinks. If only I could fly over mountains and oceans, free as the air. Then his mother tells Dodo a secret about his life and everything changes forever.

When You Heart Seeks the Sky is the story of a journey from the edges of endurance to the summits of joy. It reminds us all that we can only reach the stars by shooting for the heavens, and that dreams are what makes life worth living.

# About the Author

Wang Jian is the author of When Your Heart Seeks the Sky, a #1 runaway international bestseller for all ages. Tell your friends to visit http://www.amazon.com or http://www.bn.com and search for When Your Heart Seeks the Sky. Or you can go there yourself and place orders for additional copies to give to family and friends. Wang is a bachelor and lives with his parents in Tianjin, China. To learn more about his moving novel, visit http://www.heartseeks.com today and see how you can win a fabulous prize.

Printed in the United States
24172LVS00005B/142-186

9 781418 485986